Amy Cross is the author of more than 100 horror, paranormal, fantasy and thriller novels.

OTHER TITLES BY AMY CROSS INCLUDE

American Coven
Annie's Room
The Ash House
Asylum
B&B
The Bride of Ashbyrn House
The Camera Man
The Curse of Wetherley House
The Devil, the Witch and the Whore
Devil's Briar
The Dog
Eli's Town
The Farm
The Ghost of Molly Holt
The Ghosts of Lakeforth Hotel
The Girl Who Never Came Back
Haunted
The Haunting of Blackwych Grange
Like Stones on a Crow's Back
The Night Girl
Perfect Little Monsters & Other Stories
Stephen
The Shades
The Soul Auction
Tenderling
Ward Z

THE GHOST OF CROWFORD SCHOOL

AMY CROSS

This edition
first published by Blackwych Books Ltd
United Kingdom, 2020

Copyright © 2020 Amy Cross

All rights reserved. This book is a work of fiction. Names, characters, places, incidents and businesses are the product of the author's imagination or are used fictitiously. Any resemblance to actual persons, living or dead, or to actual events or locations, is entirely coincidental.

ISBN: 9798571501507

Also available in e-book format.

www.blackwychbooks.com

CONTENTS

PROLOGUE
page 15

CHAPTER ONE
page 25

CHAPTER TWO
page 35

CHAPTER THREE
page 45

CHAPTER FOUR
page 53

CHAPTER FIVE
page 61

CHAPTER SIX
page 71

CHAPTER SEVEN
page 79

CHAPTER EIGHT
page 87

CHAPTER NINE
page 95

CHAPTER TEN
page 103

CHAPTER ELEVEN
page 113

CHAPTER TWELVE
page 121

CHAPTER THIRTEEN
page 129

CHAPTER FOURTEEN
page 137

CHAPTER FIFTEEN
page 145

CHAPTER SIXTEEN
page 153

CHAPTER SEVENTEEN
page 161

CHAPTER EIGHTEEN
page 171

CHAPTER NINETEEN
page 179

CHAPTER TWENTY
page 187

CHAPTER TWENTY-ONE
page 195

CHAPTER TWENTY-TWO
page 203

CHAPTER TWENTY-THREE
page 211

CHAPTER TWENTY-FOUR
page 219

CHAPTER TWENTY-FIVE
page 227

CHAPTER TWENTY-SIX
page 235

CHAPTER TWENTY-SEVEN
page 243

CHAPTER TWENTY-EIGHT
page 251

CHAPTER TWENTY-NINE
page 259

CHAPTER THIRTY
page 267

CHAPTER THIRTY-ONE
page 275

CHAPTER THIRTY-TWO
page 283

CHAPTER THIRTY-THREE
page 291

CHAPTER THIRTY-FOUR
page 297

CHAPTER THIRTY-FIVE
page 307

EPILOGUE
page 315

THE GHOST OF CROWFORD SCHOOL

PROLOGUE

September 10th, 1936...

"ARE YOU SURE YOU don't want to come to the dance?" Hayley asked, stopping at the street corner and turning to see that Eve was falling further behind. "I'm sure it'll be a lot more fun than anything you've got lined up."

"I'll be there next time, I promise," Eve said cautiously, and then she glanced along the alley that led to Crowford School's imposing main building. Even at night, silhouetted against the stars, the school appeared rather ominous. She turned back to Hayley. "I hope you and the other girls enjoy yourselves."

"So where are you going instead?" Hayley

replied.

"Oh, just..."

Eve hesitated, and she was kicking herself for having not come up with a better excuse in advance. She'd just been so excited about the evening, and she'd barely been able to take her mind off her plans, even during her day teaching the second class. After a moment, she realized she was starting to blush.

"Eve Marsh," Hayley said with a smile, "if I didn't know better, I'd think you were going to meet a gentleman."

"No!" she blurted out, but she immediately realized she was turning beetroot red. Then again, in the shadows, she hoped that her face wouldn't be too visible. "I shall probably just go for a walk," she continued, "that's all. It's such a nice night, and I often enjoy taking a wander with just my thoughts for company."

"Is that right?"

Eve felt bad for lying, but she knew she didn't really have much of a choice. After all, Adam had told her most firmly that she mustn't let anyone know about their little assignations. He'd explained that he wanted to keep things under wraps, not only because of the danger that people would gossip, but also because – he claimed – he had a few enemies in the town who might take things a step too far.

"Whatever you end up doing," Hayley said after a moment, "just take care, okay? And fill me in on all the juicy details tomorrow."

"I will," Eve said. "I promise."

"Oh, so there *are* juicy details, are there?"

"No!" Eve stammered. "I mean -"

"Relax," Hayley said, interrupting her, "I'm not going to pry any further. Stay safe, though, and don't do anything I wouldn't do."

Eve watched as Hayley hurried away to join the others at the dance hall, and then – once she was sure that nobody else was around – she turned and made her way along the pitch-black alley that led through to the school's grounds. A light breeze was rustling the trees, and ordinarily Eve was the last person who'd ever venture out alone at night. Although she was twenty-three years old, she still lived with her parents and she usually preferred staying at home in the evenings. Sneaking out for the evening to meet Adam felt daring and thrilling, even though deep down she worried that she might be making a mistake.

"Just trust me," she remembered Adam telling her during their previous meeting, on the beach a week earlier. "Everything's going to be alright, but I need you to trust me."

"Of course I trust you," she'd told him. "With my whole heart."

"Then let's meet at the school next week. You've got a key, haven't you?"

Emerging from the other end of the alley, she stopped for a moment and looked around the schoolyard. During the day, the yard would be full of primary-aged children, but of course at night there was nobody to be seen. At least, not as far as Eve could tell. All she could really see was darkness, but she felt quite sure that there would be no interlopers on the school grounds so late at night. Apart from herself and Adam, at least.

She made her way toward the school building, and as she did so she reached into her pocket for the key. She'd been so proud a few months earlier, when Ms. Fletcher had entrusted her with a spare, and she felt a pang of regret as she realized that she was abusing that trust. Still, her desire to meet Adam trumped any doubts, and she had to admit that she felt a frisson of excitement as she hurried up the stone steps and stopped to unlock the door. She slid the key into the lock and gave it a turn, and then the door creaked loudly as she pushed it open. She'd never noticed before that the door was so loud, but then in the past she'd always been surrounded by loud, excited children.

"I just want to get you all to myself for a little while," Adam had whispered into her ear. His breath had felt so hot. "You can understand that, can't you?"

Once she was inside, she shut the door but left it unlocked. That had been the arrangement she'd made with Adam, but she knew she was quite early so she made her way through to room B and stopped to look at the rows of empty desks. Room B was her room, where she taught all her second year children. She allowed herself a faint smile as she made her way along the aisle that ran between the desks, and finally she reached the blackboard and saw that the day's lesson was still chalked up. She'd been teaching the children their times tables, and the class had gone rather well. Stepping back, she admired all her work, and she remembered the songs she'd taught the children to sing. Hopefully, those songs would help them remember all the complicated numbers.

Biting her bottom lip for a moment, she felt an unfamiliar sensation in her chest. It took her a moment to realize that this sensation had a name.

Pride.

She was proud.

Not of herself, of course, but of the children in her class. They were doing so well, and even the few stragglers had begun to catch up. Even little Bobby Fraser was -

Suddenly she heard the door creaking again, out in the hallway, and she turned to look back across the classroom. She listened as the door bumped shut, and then she heard footsteps echoing through the building and starting to go up the main staircase.

"Adam?" she called out, before she could stop herself. "I'm in here!"

She waited, but the footsteps continued and quickly disappeared up onto the landing. She heard Adam walking along one of the corridors, and then she made her way to the door and looked over toward the foot of the stairs.

"Adam?"

Realizing that he wouldn't possibly be able to hear her, she hurried to the stairs and began to follow him. She'd told him that they'd meet in the hallway, but he'd mentioned wanting to spend some time with her in the main hall itself, which was up on the first floor. She supposed that he must have been a little confused, and by the time she got to the top of the stairs she realized that his footsteps were indeed coming from the direction of the main hall.

"Adam!" she called out. "I'm here!"

She heard another door open, and the

footsteps continued to walk away.

Rolling her eyes, she set off after him again. She was thrilled at the prospect of seeing Adam, and she didn't mind a little chase. She'd already made up her mind that she still wasn't going to let him kiss her yet, assuming he *wanted* to kiss her, although part of her worried that she was being a little too timid. She knew that some men could be much more forward, although she felt certain that Adam was better behaved. Still, in the unlikely event that his hands began to wander, she was going to gently but firmly let him know that she wasn't that type of girl.

If he wanted real intimacy, he'd just have to wait until they were married. Not that she assumed they *would* one day get married, but...

Well, it couldn't hurt to be prepared.

In truth, she wasn't quite sure what she thought was going to happen. She was serious about Adam, though, and she could certainly imagine the *possibility* of one day becoming his wife. First, though, he would have to prove himself by courting her, and as she opened the double doors that led into the main hall she couldn't help but smile at the thought of a little romance. Adam had always been so graceful and poetic, and she saw no reason why he would ever change. And, as she closed in on her mid-twenties, Eve was starting to realize that she was something of an old-fashioned girl.

Stopping, she looked across the moonlit school hall, but there was still no sign of Adam anywhere.

"Adam?" she said cautiously. She could no longer hear any footsteps. "Adam, it's me, where are you? I'm right here."

She waited, and then she took a few steps forward. She could just about make out the stage ahead, with its rows of empty chairs arranged on either side of the desk from which Ms. Fletcher always led morning assembly. She glanced around, and then she stopped again as she tried to work out where Adam might have gone. She hadn't heard his footsteps for a minute or two by now, which meant that he couldn't have got far.

"Adam," she continued, "is this some of game? I'm afraid I'm not very good at games. I've told you that before, haven't I? Come on, we don't have much time, I have to be home in two hours. Let's not mess around with silliness."

She paused, listening for some sign of him.

"I want to see you," she added with a nervous smile. "I want to -"

Before she could get another word out, she gasped as she felt a hand on her waist from behind.

She began to turn, but then she froze as she felt a kiss on the side of her neck, and a moment later she saw another hand reaching around, holding a single, beautiful red rose.

"Oh, Adam," she said, with tears in her eyes, as she took the rose, carefully avoiding the many thorns on its stem, "you shouldn't have. No-one has ever bought me a rose before."

She turned the rose around for a moment, and then – out of nowhere – she came to a decision that she found quite shocking. She decided that, contrary to everything she'd told herself over the previous few days, she *was* going to let him kiss her after all. Nothing too deep, of course, but certainly more than a peck on the cheek. The last thing she wanted was to seem cold or uninterested, so if he tried to use his tongue, she would let him. She felt a shiver run through her bones at the prospect, but she told herself that it was time to be brave.

Heart heart was pounding.

"Adam," she said cautiously, "I think -"

Suddenly she let out a pained gasp as a knife burst into her back and out through the center of her chest. Looking down, she saw the tip glinting in the low light, and blood was already dripping down from the blade. She tried to cry out, but somehow she found that she could barely make a sound at all, and she realized she could feel blood soaking the front of her dress. And then, just as she managed to let out a faint groan, she felt another sharp pain as the knife was twisted from behind.

"No!" she sobbed, already feeling the life drain from her body as her knees began to buckle. "Please, no..."

CHAPTER ONE

May 15th, 1988...

"ALRIGHT THERE!" MR. KEPPER shouted, watching the boys race across the yard for a moment before putting the whistle in his mouth and blowing. "That's enough! Red team, you get a penalty!"

"Why?" Christian yelled, stopping and turning to look over at his P.E. teacher. "That was never a foul!"

"You grabbed him from behind," Mr. Kepper replied.

"That was an accident!"

"I don't care." He blew the whistle again, before pointing toward the penalty spot. "Come on,

I want to get this wrapped up. Who's going to take it?"

The boys starting talking among themselves, although Christian was still grumbling as he trudged over to join his teammates. They were almost at the end of the last class of the day, and that meant there was precious little time left to save the match. Although he was only eleven years old, Christian had an almighty competitive streak and he absolutely hated the idea of losing. Even if it was only a stupid P.E. football match that didn't actually mean anything.

"Have you picked someone yet?" Mr. Kepper called out, before hurrying over to the gaggle of boys and tapping one of them on the shoulder. "Bradley, you're up."

Bradley turned to him.

"But -"

"My decision is final," Mr. Kepper continued, shoving him toward the penalty spot with such force that Bradley almost tripped and fell. He checked his watch. "This is more or less going to be the last touch of the game, Mr. Firth, so make it count."

Realizing that there was no point arguing with Mr. Kepper, Bradley made his way over to the penalty spot, where Simon had already set the ball down.

"Good luck," Simon said, without sounding too confident, as he left Bradley to face the goalkeeper alone.

"This is your one chance at redemption, boy," Mr. Kepper said, before holding the whistle up. "Everyone's watching, and your team are depending on you. Try not to screw it up."

As soon as the whistle blew, Bradley told himself that he just had to strike. He could see Wayne Cooper hopping about on the goal-line, trying to cause a distraction, but he took a deep breath and tried to ignore all that silliness. He focused for a moment, and finally he ran toward the spot and kicked the ball as hard as he could.

***

"That was *rubbish*," Simon said a short while later, as they headed across the yard at the end of the day. "That was, without a doubt, the worst penalty I've ever seen anyone take in my entire life."

"It wasn't that bad," Bradley protested.

"It's still in the tree!"

"Everyone misses occasionally," Bradley pointed out. "Even John Aldridge misses sometimes."

"You're no John Aldridge," Simon said with a chuckle. "Don't worry, though. I'll still pick you for our team next week."

"You'll have to," Christian added, "because I won't. Don't worry, though, Bradley, you're not the worst player in the school. Just, I don't know, the second or third worst."

"Thanks," Bradley muttered, before all three boys stopped as they heard the sound of breaking glass nearby.

A moment later, Charles Oliver and his friends ran into view, hurrying out from behind the back of the old, abandoned main building. They raced across the yard, before stopping to get their breath back.

"What were you doing back there?" Christian asked them.

"Liam dared me to throw a rock at one of the windows," Charles explained, "and I did!"

"I didn't mean you were supposed to *break* a window," Liam told him.

"How can I throw a rock at the window and not break it, dummy?" Charles asked, clipping him around the ear. "That's the whole point of it!"

"You were only supposed to get her attention, that's all," Liam said.

"Get attention from who?" Bradley asked.

"Who do you think?" Charles turned to him. "You know there's a ghost in there, don't you?"

Bradley and the others turned and looked at the old building. Ever since Crowford School's new, purpose-built classrooms had been opened some time in the previous decade, the original school had stood empty and abandoned at the far end of the yard. There was talk of the building eventually getting demolished, to make way for flats. The lower windows had been boarded up, but the windows on the upper floor had been left as they were, although there was no way of seeing anything inside. The windows merely reflected the gray sky and the tops of nearby trees, although somehow that made the whole place seem even creepier.

"Her name," Charles continued, putting one arm around Bradley's shoulder and one arm around Christian's, "was Eve Marsh, and she was murdered in there a long time ago. I think it was in the 1930's. Anyway, she was murdered by her boyfriend, and her body was left all cut up in pieces in the old hall. Someone found it the next day, and ever since her ghost has walked the corridors. Apparently that's the main reason the building was abandoned, and why they want to knock it down. It's said that when teachers tried to hold classes in there, Eve Marsh used to make all the doors bang shut."

"You're making all of that up," Christian told him.

"No, I heard it too," Liam said. "Everyone knows about Eve Marsh. She was killed by her boyfriend, and he was never caught. He pretended his name was Adam, but that was just a fake one."

"They say that even now, her face is sometimes seen at one of the windows," Charles said, pulling Simon and Christian closer as they all looked over at the building. "Not often, but sometimes. That's why the lower windows were boarded up, to make it harder to spot her. And when she appears, it's a sign that something really bad is about to happen in Crowford."

"Have *you* seen her?" Bradley asked cautiously.

"No, but my mum's boyfriend has."

Bradley turned to him.

"His name's Steve, and he reckons when he was a pupil here, he saw her twice. Both times, there was a tragedy not long after. The first time, another pupil got hit on the level crossing on his way home from school and he died. That's definitely true, you can ask anyone. And the second time, there was a car crash a few days later, and someone died in that too. Steve says he saw Eve Marsh's face at the window both times, and she was staring down straight at him."

"That's a load of rubbish," Bradley said, although his voice betrayed a certain hesitancy as he – and the others – continued to look at the building. "If there was actually a ghost in there, after all this time, someone would have done something about it."

"Ghostbusters aren't a real thing," Charles explained. "What else could they do, except lock the building up and ignore it? And wait for it to get knocked down, obviously. All the teachers know it's true, but they won't admit it. Did you know that Mr. Ripple used to have hair? It all fell out after he saw Eve Marsh's ghost. Now they're just waiting for the place to get demolished, and then they hope the ghost will be gone forever."

They all stood and watched the building in silence. Each boy had his gaze fixed on one of the windows, just in case a ghostly face appeared. No-one wanted to be the next to say anything, and they were each secretly convinced that soon a face *would* appear, and that they'd see the ghostly figure of Eve Marsh staring back out at them. Bradley, in particular, was holding his breath in anticipation, and he could feel a growing sense of fear starting to twist in the pit of his belly.

"Seeya, losers!" Charles yelled suddenly,

patting them both hard on the back before turning and hurrying away with his friends close behind. "Don't let the ghost of Eve Marsh get you!"

"He's such an idiot," Bradley muttered, although he was still watching the building.

"You know what we should do?" Christian said. He waited for either Simon or Bradley to reply, and then he rolled his eyes. "This is our last term at Crowford School, so it's almost our last chance. Before we leave, we should totally go in there and try to find that ghost."

"You're crazy," Bradley told him.

"No, I'm brave," Christian replied.

"Ghosts don't exist," Bradley added.

"Then what's crazy about going in there? Why would you be scared of going into that building if you're so sure that ghosts aren't real?" He paused. "In fact, why don't we go round the back right now? We won't go in, not yet, but we can at least take a look."

"I don't want to," Bradley said.

"Because you know that there's a real chance you might see the ghost of Eve Marsh?"

Bradley turned to him, still trying to think of an excuse, but then he heard the honk of a car horn. Looking the other way, he saw his dad's car parked at the side of the road, and he realized he had to get going.

"Are you visiting her tonight?" Christian asked. "Don't you normally go on Mondays and Thursdays?"

"She wasn't feeling well yesterday, so we're going today instead," Bradley replied, setting off toward the car before turning to his friends again. "Might see you tomorrow."

"Good luck," Christian said, with a hint of sadness in his voice. "I mean that."

"Thanks," Bradley said, although he could feel a heavy sense of dread in his chest. "I'd better go."

With that, he ran off across the yard, leaving his friends to look back up at the old school building and wonder about what might be lurking in its long-abandoned rooms.

CHAPTER TWO

"DAD," BRADLEY SAID AS he sat in the front passenger seat and watched the road ahead, "can I ask you something?"

"What?" Dave replied.

Bradley turned to him. He'd been wanting to ask one particular question ever since he'd climbed into the car, but he'd hesitated since he didn't want to sound like a complete idiot. Now, however, he was unable to hold back for even a moment longer.

"Do you believe in ghosts?"

"Of course I don't," Dave said, keeping his eyes on the road. "Why would you even ask? Have you finished reading your comic?"

Bradley looked down at the comic in his lap. It was one of those smaller American comics that were always left in a random pile in the paper shop; there was never any guarantee of what would be in the pile, so sometimes he'd miss a few issues of a comic he was trying to collect. He'd tried to concentrate on the story, but for once he was having trouble. He started flicking through the comic again, hoping to distract himself by reading the letters page, and then he turned back to his father.

"You know the old school?" he asked.

"I do."

"Do you think it's haunted?"

"How could it be haunted?"

"Someone told me that a woman got murdered there years ago. Is that true?"

"Of course it's..." Dave's voice trailed off for a moment. "We're nearly at the hospital. You should try to finish your comic."

"But did a woman really get murdered at the old school?"

"Not in my lifetime."

"What about before you were born?"

His father took a moment to indicate, and then he changed lanes, preparing to take the turn-off that led to the hospital.

"There's no point talking about ghosts," he said finally, still watching the road. "You need to focus on things that are actually real, like your homework. I noticed your grades are slipping. When we get home later, I want to see your homework diary. It's about time you got better at organizing things. And as for ghosts, don't be stupid, okay? I don't want you to talk about things like that again."

***

"It all depends on what the doctors say later," Bradley's mother Debbie said, as she squeezed his hand. She was sitting up in her hospital bed, with a scarf wrapped around her bald head. "If they say I'm in remission, I'll be able to come home for a while."

"How many times have you been in remission now?" Bradley asked.

"I've lost count."

"And you always..."

His voice trailed off as he saw all the bruises on her arm from where needles had been inserted. The bruises were all sorts of different colors; some where dark, almost black, while others were a kind of sickly yellow. They looked like little galaxies painted on her arm.

Looking up at her face, he saw her bloodied, chapped lips.

"If I get out tomorrow," Debbie continued, "I think we should think about doing something really fun at the weekend. How about getting ice cream on the pier? I know this is going to sound silly, but there have been times over the past few weeks when I've really craved ice cream on the pier. Or, if want to be a little more adventurous, we could go for a drive and just see where we end up."

He stared at her chapped lips for a moment longer, and he wondered whether ice cream might hurt her. Then again, he knew better than to ask, since he didn't want to make her feel bad. Besides, deep down he knew that however bad things might seem, his mother would always pull through. She'd been battling leukemia for over a year now, almost eighteen months, and things had looked pretty bad before.

But she always pulled through.

"I think a drive might be a really good idea," she said. "There are plenty of little villages near Crowford that I've never been to. Why don't we go and explore?"

He paused, not wanting to admit that he was worried about the idea of being alone with her. What if they went out and something bad happened? Suddenly, realizing that he needed to give her an answer, he nodded.

"I'm going to go down to the cafe and get some coffee," Dave said, letting out a loud sigh as he got to his feet. "Anyone else want anything?"

Bradley shook his head.

"We're good, thanks," Debbie said as Dave shuffled out of the room.

"Mum," Bradley said, turning to his mother once he was sure his father was out of earshot, "do you believe in ghosts?"

She furrowed her brow.

"Some people were talking at school today," he continued. "Do you know the old building that's abandoned now? The one that used to be the main school?"

"Sure."

"Did *you* go to school there?"

"No, I went to Crowford Parochial." She paused. "Why?"

"It's just that some people were saying that the old building at Crowford School is..."

His voice trailed off for a moment.

"Is it true that someone was murdered there?" he asked finally.

"Well, I don't..." She hesitated. "You know, now that you mention it, I think I remember hearing something about it. When I worked on the paper, there was some talk about someone who died there, but it was a very long time ago, sweetheart. There's no need to worry about it now."

"But a woman *was* murdered there?"

"It was so long ago. I think it was the 1930's, some time like that."

"And it really happened?"

"I really don't remember the details. I know there was some talk about the case a few years ago, when there was some anniversary. I think it was fifty years after it happened, and we had a feature about it in the paper. Like I said, there's no need to be scared. It happened so long ago."

"But that's exactly the point," he continued. "It happened fifty years ago, but people still see her face at the windows."

"Well, I'm not sure that's quite true," she said cautiously. "Sweetheart, people say a lot of things, but sometimes they're not true."

"What if this *is* true, though?" he asked. "Charles Oliver says her name was Eve Marsh and she murdered by her boyfriend and she was chopped up into pieces and now her ghost is there and -"

"Hold on, there," Debbie said, interrupting him, "I think you're getting a little carried away. And why are you and your friends talking about something so horrible, anyway?" Spotting the comic he'd set down on the table, she picked it up and began to flick through the pages, only to stop as soon as she saw a panel showing a man being torn about by spiders. "Bradley," she continued, "does your father know that you're reading this sort of thing?"

"There's nothing wrong with it," he replied, reaching out to take the comic, but then pausing as he watched her checking out the rest of the pages. "It's not scary."

"It's a little bit too much for you," she said, horrified by some of the images she was seeing. After reaching the end of the comic, she closed it and set it down. "Have you been reading these for a while? Have your friends been reading them too? Is this why you're suddenly talking about ghosts and murders?"

"No, that was just because Charles -"

"I'm going to have to talk to your father," she continued, "because I think maybe you're a little too young to be reading these particular comics. And I want you to promise me something, Bradley. I want you to stop worrying about that old school building, okay?"

"But -"

"I want you to stop even thinking about it," she said firmly. "Anything that happened there, happened a long time ago, and it's firmly in the past." She paused for a moment, watching his expression, waiting to see how he was going to react. "Do you understand, Bradley?" she added. "That abandoned building is *just* an abandoned building. There's no such thing as ghosts."

***

A short while later, sitting out in the corridor, Bradley was just about able to hear his parents talking in the hospital room.

"I don't want him reading this type of material," his mother was saying, keeping her voice down a little. "He's too young to be reading comics about people being eaten and slaughtered like this. He should still be on the *Beano* and the *Dandy*. *Transformers*, maybe."

"He's eleven," his father replied, sounding a little frustrated. "I'm sure he's seen far worse."

"I don't care," she replied, "I'm putting my foot down on this, okay? It's already started to affect him, he's talking about all these horrible things that happened years ago in Crowford. Please, Dave, there's only so much I can do from here. I need you to be on my side."

"Fine," his father muttered. "I'll make sure

he doesn't buy them again."

Bradley looked down at his hands and tried to ignore the flicker of irritation that was stirring in his belly. He knew that the comic had nothing to do with his interest in the abandoned school building, and he couldn't help thinking about the windows on the building's top floor. Why were his parents so determined to deny the possibility of a ghost?

CHAPTER THREE

"YEAH, SHE MIGHT BE coming home tomorrow," Bradley said as he sat at the bottom of the stairs, talking on the phone. "She's got to talk to the doctor first."

"That's good news," Christian replied. "So listen, after you left earlier, Simon and I were talking and we came up with a plan. We think we should try to get into the old school building and find out if Eve Marsh's ghost is really in there."

"And how are you going to do that?"

"We'll find a way."

"I'm pretty sure it's kept locked all the time."

"So we'll have to be inventive," Christian continued. "It's not every day that an actual haunted house, or building, drops into your lap. This might be the only one we ever get to see, so we have to seize the opportunity. Are you with us, or are you against us?"

"Tea'll be ready in five minutes," his grandmother said, leaning through from the front room. "Are you two still talking about homework?"

Bradley nodded, hoping that she hadn't overheard any of the conversation.

"Well, wrap it up in the next five minutes," she told him, as she turned and headed back through to the kitchen. "You don't want your tea to get cold, do you?"

"No, Nana," he replied.

"And that phone bill keeps creeping up each month."

"We have to do it on a weekend," Christian said. "Preferably in the evening, so that it's dark outside. We can't do it *this* weekend, because we need time to prepare, but next weekend's a possibility. Simon and I made a list of equipment we should take with us."

"What kind of equipment?" Bradley asked.

"Standard ghost-hunting things. Like a camera, for one thing. Simon's got a disposable one he got for his birthday and he's only used about half the film, so he's going to save the rest. And I've got a tape recorder. I just need to get some new batteries for it. What can you bring to the table, Bradley?"

"I'm not even sure that this is a good idea," he said cautiously. "Mum didn't seem very keen."

"But she confirmed that the stories are true, right?"

"She said a woman definitely got murdered there, about fifty years ago, but she said she isn't still there as a ghost. She said ghosts don't exist."

"Then she shouldn't have any problem with us doing this," Christian pointed out, "not if there's not a ghost, because that means it's not dangerous. We're not going to tell anyone, though. You know what parents are like. So how about it? Are you up for some ghost-hunting next weekend?"

***

"Nana, do you know anything about the woman who was murdered in the old school?"

As she finished dishing up beans on toast, Josephine turned to her grandson. She hesitated for a moment, and then she turned back to the cooker and spooned out some more beans.

"If you mean Eve Marsh," she said after a few seconds, "then yes, as it happens, I do. Ms. Marsh was my teacher the year before."

"You went to Crowford School?"

"I did." She carried two plates over to the table. "Ms. Marsh was a very nice woman. In fact, I think she was my favorite teacher from back then." She took a seat opposite Bradley. "We were all so very sad about what happened to her. My friends and I would have been nine years old, I believe. We were just old enough to understand that something very nasty had occurred."

"Because she was cut up, right? Into little pieces?"

"That's not what happened."

"Then what did?"

"She was stabbed, I believe. Multiple times."

"By her boyfriend?"

"I don't think the perpetrator was ever caught. There was some talk that she'd had a boyfriend, but as far as I recall no-one had ever met him. You must remember, back then the police didn't have all the resources that they have today, so I imagine the investigation didn't go too far." She took a scrunched piece of tissue from her right sleeve and wiped her mouth, before putting the tissue back. "It was all very sad, though. We had to take a week off school, because the hall and some of the classrooms were a crime scene. Now, eat your tea before it gets cold."

Bradley did as he was told, but in truth he still had a whole lot of questions.

"After she was dead," he said cautiously, "did you ever hear anything strange about the school?"

"Such as?"

"Such as..."

He hesitated, worried that his grandmother – like his parents – would dismiss the idea of a ghost out of hand.

"Did doors get banged while you were there?"

"Doors?"

"Like an invisible force was doing stuff."

"Of course not," she replied. "Nothing like that happened. Why? Have you been hearing stories?"

"Someone said that she's been seen since she died," he told her. "Someone said that she's haunting the school."

"Well, you mustn't listen to that kind of nonsense," she replied tersely. "If you ask me, there are too many bored people in this town, Bradley, and they let their minds get up to all sorts of nonsense."

"But if a ghost -"

"Stop it!" she snapped angrily, setting her

knife and fork down. "Do you hear me? There's no ghost at that school, and the only people who believe in that foolishness are people with weak minds. Do you have a weak mind, Bradley?"

"No," he said quietly, already regretting the fact that he'd raised the subject.

"I don't want to hear another word about ghosts," she continued, "do you understand? Ms. Marsh was a wonderful woman and a very good teacher and what happened to her was a tragedy, but there's absolutely no truth to any claim that she's still there. People just die, and they're gone." She stared at him for a moment, her eyes wild with anger. "Don't you think the poor woman suffered enough, without having her death turned into some lurid spectacle?"

"Yes," he murmured. "I'm sorry."

"I might have been young when it all happened, but I still remember the way her death gripped the town. For a while, it was all that anyone could talk about. Even a few years later, people just went on and on about the whole thing. I'm not a fan of mindless titillation, Bradley, and you shouldn't be either."

"I'm not."

"I mean every word," she said firmly, as the phone began to rang in the hallway. She got to her feet. "I don't want to hear anything more about it, do you understand? Not one word!"

"Okay," he said as she headed through to answer the phone. "I get it."

He began to eat his beans on toast, although he was a little startled by the way that his grandmother had exploded while they'd been talking about the dead woman. She was always so calm and reserved, so he couldn't help but wonder why she'd been so uptight after he'd started talking about Eve Marsh. His parents had been skeptical, but not in an angry way, and Bradley couldn't help but wonder whether he'd accidentally touched upon a subject that made his grandmother feel particularly furious.

A moment later, hearing her coming back through, he pretended to be entirely focused on his tea.

"That was your mother, calling from the hospital," Josephine said, as she sat back down opposite. She seemed a little troubled by something, and then she took out her tissue and wiped her mouth again. "The doctors say she's in remission. She's coming home tomorrow for at least a week or two. Isn't that wonderful news?"

"Can I stay home from school?" he asked.

"Not a chance, young man," she replied

firmly. "Now finish your tea, do the washing up, and then go up to do your homework."

They ate the rest of the meal in silence. Once they were both done, Bradley washed up all the pots, plates and cutlery and lined them up to dry, and then he went to his room and tried to focus on the sums he needed to have ready for the following day. His mind kept wandering, not only because of the supposed ghost in the old building, but also because he was excited about his mother coming home the next day. He knew he shouldn't get his hopes up, but he couldn't help thinking that this time – just maybe – she'd never have to go back into hospital again.

Down in the kitchen, meanwhile, Josephine had taken a small box from the dresser and opened it on the table. She sorted through the various trinkets and photos inside, before unfolding one particular picture, which showed a group of schoolchildren standing in a yard and smiling. At the middle of the front row, Eve Marsh was grinning at the camera, and Josephine felt a few tears in her eyes as she thought back to the awful days and weeks following the murder.

"It wasn't fair," she whispered to herself quietly. "That bastard should never have been allowed to get away with it."

CHAPTER FOUR

"GOT EVERYTHING?" DAVE SAID the following morning as he switched the engine off and turned to see that Debbie was already climbing out of the car. "Are you sure you don't want me to help you carry your bags in?"

"Best not," she replied, hauling her bags off the back seat and setting them down on the pavement, and then leaning back down to look into the car. "Thank you for the lift."

"How are you feeling?" he asked.

"Like a woman who's just gone through several more bouts of chemo," she said, "but who, all things considered, isn't doing too badly. Don't worry, I won't strain myself, but I won't just sit around wrapped in cotton wool, either. There's no way I'm willing to waste my time back out in the real world."

"What did the doctor say?"

"I told you, I'm in remission. I know that doesn't mean I'm cured, I know I've been in remission a few times before, but I'm well enough for them to let me come home. I specifically asked them if I could go out and about, and they told me that it's fine. I'm even allowed to drive!"

"You need to rest."

"Now you sound like my mother," she said, rolling her eyes. "Thanks again for the lift, Dave."

She began to swing the door shut.

"We could go somewhere at the weekend," he said suddenly.

She sighed.

"You, me and Bradley," he continued. "Don't dismiss the idea out of hand, it could be fun. You probably don't feel much like driving at the moment, so I could take us out to lunch at a pub in one of the villages."

"Thank you," she replied, "but no."

"Why not?"

"I just don't think that it's a good idea," she told him. "I'll give you a call over the weekend to let you know when's a good day for you to see Bradley at the start of the week."

She hesitated, and then she slammed the door shut.

Dave sat and watched as she carried her

bags inside. Josephine appeared in the doorway a moment later and immediately grabbed the bags, before ushering her daughter into the house and closing the door. For a few seconds, Dave simply sat all alone, before reaching out to start the engine again.

***

"I simply refuse to allow you to do anything today," Josephine said as she steered Debbie toward the kitchen table. "I don't care what you think, you're going to put your feet up."

"Mum, I'm fine," she replied, although she knew better than to argue. She took a seat, and then she winced slightly as she felt a slight pain in her side. She quickly tried to cover the fact that she was in any discomfort, but she could already tell that her mother had noticed.

"What's wrong?"

"Nothing, Mum."

"Debbie, if -"

"I'm fine," she added, trying not to sound too impatient. "Please don't over-analyze every little thing that I do. Doctor Sanders never would have let me come home if he didn't think I was up to it, and I've got an appointment next week with Doctor Frazer at the surgery. I've got plenty of people keeping tabs on me. I just want things to be normal while I'm here." She sighed. "Please, Mum, I just had this exact conversation with Dave on the way from the hospital. I don't need to have it again with you."

"You look well."

"I look like crap." She paused. "But I hopefully look better than I have for a while, so I'll take that. Now, was that offer of a cup of tea just a tease, or am I really in with a chance?"

"Do you have much washing? Never mind, I can do all of that this afternoon, while you watch TV."

"Actually, I'm meeting Julie Raskin in town."

"You are not!"

"I am, Mum," Debbie said firmly. "Just for a coffee and a catch-up. I might only have fourteen days at home, and I want to make the most of that. I want to see my friends."

"I'll come with you, then."

"You bloody well won't," Debbie replied, before sighing. "Can I just be normal for at least a couple of weeks, Mum? I want to catch up with Julie and have a natter and not have someone fussing over me for an hour or two. I called her from the hospital and arranged this meeting already, and she was going into town early to do some other things, so I can't even get in touch with her now to cancel. I'm meeting her!"

"I need to go to a few shops," Josephine muttered, heading over to put the kettle on. "I'll walk into town with you, at least. No arguments."

"Fine," Debbie said, as she saw one of her mother's boxes on the table. Reaching over, she opened the lid, and she was surprised to find an old school photo on top of all the other items. Holding the photo up, she saw her mother's nine-year-old face smiling out from the picture. "Thinking about the past, huh?"

Josephine turned to her and immediately froze.

"Oh, that," she stammered, "it's just..."

"That's the teacher who died, isn't it?" Debbie continued. "Eve Marsh? Sorry, she's fresh in my memory because Bradley was talking about her yesterday when he came to the hospital. Apparently he and his friends heard all the lurid details about what happened. You know what kids are like, they love anything that's even slightly gory."

"It's not appropriate for them to talk about her," Josephine replied, hurrying over and taking the photo from Debbie, and then putting it into the box, which she quickly slid back into the dresser drawer.

"I was only -"

"Bradley should know better than to take an interest in something so awful," Josephine continued, clearly irritated. "If you ask me, he spends far too much time watching the television and reading comics, his brain's going to rot if he keeps that up. Children these days have far too much freedom."

Debbie watched as her mother headed back over to the kettle, which was slowly starting to boil.

"You remember Eve Marsh, don't you?" she asked finally.

"She was my teacher for a year," Josephine replied, with her back to Debbie now as she put tea bags into two cups.

"Do you remember there being a lot of talk at the time?" Debbie continued. "About what really happened, I mean. About that Adam guy that she was supposed to be meeting."

"I can't say that I do."

"You know, when I was working on the paper, I heard quite a lot of gossip. Stuff that we could never print in a million years, but..." She paused. "The way I understand it, everyone knows *exactly* who killed Eve Marsh. It was -"

"Do we really have to talk about this right now?"

"It's been a long time. Don't you think the truth should come out?"

"I don't see what good it would do to rake things up."

"But the truth, Mum... I mean, a woman was murdered. Maybe more than one. Don't you think that subsequent generations have a duty to at least set the record straight if we can? From what I heard, there's really no doubt about who did it, and it's not like there's even anyone around who can be hurt by the truth anymore. The guy who killed her is still alive, and if there's even a chance that he can be brought to justice, then -"

"Actually, that's where you're wrong," Josephine said, turning to her. "He died a few months ago. I'm not surprised that you missed the news, but the fact of the matter is that he's gone, so there's really nothing to gain by digging it all up again." She took a deep breath, and now there were tears in her eyes.

"Mum, are you okay?"

"I just don't think this is what we should be talking about. Especially not today of all days." Josephine closed her eyes for a moment as she tried to pull herself together. When she opened them again, tears were still glistening. "I don't know why people always want to drag up these awful things," she continued finally. "When something's over, it's over. There's no-one left who could possibly benefit from the truth coming out now, so what's the point? We should be focusing on nice things, and on the future, rather than dwelling on the more sordid aspects of Crowford's history."

"A woman was murdered," Debbie muttered under her breath, as her mother turned back to the tea cups. "If it was me, I know I'd want the perpetrator to be brought to justice. And if that wasn't possible, then I'd at least want everyone to know the truth."

CHAPTER FIVE

PUTTING THE WHISTLE IN his mouth, Mr. Kepper blew hard as he marched across the grass.

"Great," Christian said, rolling his eyes as he turned to Bradley. "Here he comes again."

"What are you boys doing over here?" the teacher asked as he reached them. "I told you to stick close to the playground."

"We thought we might get some better specimens here," Bradley said, holding up the mason jar he'd been given at the start of class. "We thought it'd be boring if we all get leaves from the same part of the school grounds."

Looking past Mr. Kepper, he saw the rest of the class collecting leaves from the far edge of the playground.

"Leaves are leaves," Charles said, holding

up part of a plant that he'd just pulled out of the ground. "They're all stupid, and they're all the same."

"You think so, do you?" Mr. Kepper asked.

"I can tell just by looking at them."

"Well, that's where you're wrong, young man. The whole point of this experiment is for you to see that while there are underlying similarities, each plant has developed its own unique way of adapting to its environment. Just because they're all green, that doesn't mean that these leaves are all the same."

"If you say so," Charles muttered.

"Don't try to be smart with me, young man," Mr. Kepper said firmly.

"I'm bored," Charles replied. "I need the toilet. Can I go to the toilet, please?"

"You're just trying to get out of doing this project."

"No, Sir, I really need the toilet," he said, and he began to squirm uncomfortably on the spot. He was, however, smiling slightly. "Or do you want me to wet myself?"

The other boys began to giggle.

Sighing, Mr. Kepper looked around, and then he reached into his pockets and pulled out a set of keys.

"Fine, Charles," he said, as he slid one particular key off the chain and held it out to him.

"If you need to go to the toilet so badly, you can go to the *nearest* toilet. Which happens to be behind you."

"Huh?"

Charles turned, and his smile faded as soon as he saw the old school building. He and the others had strayed far from the new building, almost all the way across the field, and when Charles turned back to looked at his teacher he saw the slightly rusty key that was being offered to him.

"You forget," Mr. Kepper said, "that I'm a fire warden, which means I have a key to every door on school property. The toilets in the new block are a shade over five hundred meters from here, whereas the ones in the old building are only about sixty meters away. If you're so absolutely desperate to go to the toilet, Charles, then I'm sure you'll want to avail yourself of the closest facilities, won't you?"

"Well..." Charles stared at the key for a moment. "Actually, it's okay, I think I don't need to go after all."

"Nonsense," Mr. Kepper replied, stepping over to him and pressing the key into his hand. "We really don't want you to have an accident, do we?"

The other boys laughed again, although they were a little nervous this time.

"So what's it to be?" the teacher continued. "You're not going to be a little coward in front of your friends, are you? Or are you a chicken after all?"

***

As he slid the key into the lock of the old building's front door, Charles swallowed hard. He was hoping that the key wouldn't work, but it fitted perfectly, and a moment later he gave it a turn and he heard the door unlock. In that moment, he felt his chest tighten with nerves, but when he looked over his shoulder and saw Mr. Kepper and the others watching him from the grass, he knew he couldn't back out.

He looked at the door again and saw that all the paint was flaking off. He took a deep breath, telling himself not to be scared, and then he slowly opened the door.

As soon as he looked into the main entrance hallway, he felt a burst of fear in his chest. The place was a dump, with patches of wallpaper that looked to have been scratched from the walls, while the floor was littered with dirt and dead leaves. There was a stale, slightly rotten smell in the air, and the stench only became more overpowering as Charles forced himself to take a step forward. A floorboard creaked loudly beneath his left foot, announcing his arrival, and when he looked at the large central staircase he couldn't help but feel as if some kind of presence was waiting for him. He looked up at the top of the staircase, and he swallowed hard as he thought of all the dark, empty rooms in the rest of the building.

He looked over his shoulder and saw the others still by the bushes, where they were supposed to be collecting specimens.

Mr. Kepper, grinning from ear to ear, waved at him.

Charles hesitated, and then he turned and stepped further into the hallway.

"First corridor to the left," he remembered Mr. Kepper telling him. "Far end. You'll find a rather grim but fully functional bathroom. What's wrong, Mr. Oliver? You're not scared, are you?"

And then, somewhat unbelievably, Mr. Kepper had made a chicken noise and flapped his elbows like wings.

Charles had denied being scared, of course, because there was no way he'd been willing to admit to any weakness in front of the others. He knew how fast a story like that could spread through the playground. Now, however, as he looked along the corridor and saw a door at the far end, he had to admit that he regretted faking the need to go to the toilet. He hadn't even faked it that well, either, because Mr. Kepper had totally been onto him.

"Oh," his teacher had added, "and just in case you think you can take a pee just inside the doorway, or just not take one at all, I want you to tell me what color the toilet is. So we know you went all the way."

"Stupid idiot," Charles muttered under his breath, before setting off along the corridor. Almost every other board creaked beneath his feet, and he kept looking all around as he passed a row of empty classrooms. "He's probably not allowed to send me in here anyway. I'm going to tell Mummy and Daddy about this and get him into so much trouble."

The empty classrooms were even creepier than the hallway. Old desks had been left behind in some, although there were no chairs.

By the time he got to the end of the corridor, he was feeling a little braver. A *little*. The old school wasn't so scary, not now he was getting used to it, although he felt a flicker of fear as he saw another, smaller staircase winding up toward the upper floor. He was tempted to go up there and take a look, just so he could brag to the others that he'd gone exploring the whole building, but then he figured he could do that anyway. No-one would know if he lied.

He headed over to the nearby door and pushed it open, and he grimaced as soon as he saw a single, foul, pale green toilet.

"Nice," he muttered, before shutting the door and turning to head back the way he came.

At least, he figured, he'd be able to wipe the

smile of Mr. Kepper's face by telling him the correct color.

Stopping suddenly, he saw that one of the nearby walls was covered in thick scratches. He stepped closer, and he felt a shudder run through his chest as he saw that the scratches spelled out a name, over and over, in different sizes. The name had been carved all over the wall, even high up near the ceiling, and even low down on the skirting board.

"Adam," Charles whispered, stepping back and looking around to see that the same name had been scratched into the wall hundreds of times.

Now that he'd noticed the name on one wall, he began to notice it on others as well. As he looked all around, he realized that someone had scratched the name Adam into almost every surface, even on the walls running up along the side of the staircase. He was sure that he'd have noticed something like that before, but he figured that perhaps he'd missed all the scratches in the gloom. And then, just as he was starting to tell himself that there was no need to worry, he realized he could hear a faint scratching sound coming from back along the corridor, from the entrance hallway.

He froze, listening as the sound continued, trying to make himself believe that it was something else.

"Hello?" he whispered, although he stopped

himself from saying anything else. For a couple of seconds, at least. "I'm not scared, you know," he continued, unable to stop himself as he imagined someone hiding and preparing to jump out at him. "This is just a stinky old building, and it's completely empty."

Finally, realizing that he just had to get back outside, he began to make his way along the corridor. He once again passed the abandoned classrooms, and when he glanced through the windows he saw that the name Adam was even scratched into the glass. He stopped at one of the doors and saw the name Adam etched into all the walls of room B. He was sure he'd looked into that room a few minutes earlier, and that the walls had been dirty but untouched.

He swallowed hard, and then he started walking again.

The scratching sound was continuing up ahead, meanwhile, and he slowed as he edged closer to the hallway. For the first time, he was starting to notice how cold the school felt, as if there was ice in the air.

Reaching the hallway, he looked around. The scratching continued, but now it seemed to be coming from somewhere upstairs. He looked over at the large staircase, and at the emptiness up on the landing. And then, in an instant, the scratching stopped.

He waited, not even daring to breathe.

A moment later, he heard a floorboard creaking somewhere over his shoulder. He turned, not really expecting to see anything, only to spot a woman standing at the far end of the corridor.

***

"He's probably taking a dump," Christian said as he held up another leaf and saw ants scurrying across its lower end. "Have you seen how many bags of crisps he has every morning? It's amazing he can even walk with all that -"

Before he could get another word out, they all heard a scream in the distance. Turning, they were just in time to see Charles racing from the old school building and running away across the lawn.

"Charles!" Mr. Kepper called out, before setting off after him. He started furiously blowing his whistle. "Mr. Oliver, get back here this instant!"

CHAPTER SIX

"NOT A LOT HAS changed," Julie pointed out, as she and Debbie sat by the window in a cafe opposite the pier. "Life moves slowly in Crowford."

"I don't mind that at the moment," Debbie replied, watching as a young couple made their way across the road. "It feels like only yesterday that *we* were the kids in town, racing around and causing trouble."

"Do you remember how we used to get Colin to serve us in the Star and Garter?" Julie asked. "That was the only pub in town where we could get a drink before we were legal. He served me once when I was fourteen! He just didn't care, did he? You'd never get away with something like that now." She paused. "Hey, we should totally have a pub crawl some time. You and me, and the girls.

The Star, the Cow, the Hoy, the Crest, all the old haunts."

"Maybe," Debbie said cautiously.

"Are you not allowed to drink?"

"It's complicated," Debbie replied. "Hey, not to change the subject, but do you remember we ran an article about that Eve Marsh murder when we were at the paper?"

"Vaguely. Maybe. Why?"

"I was thinking about it, that's all. I remember Lou was very careful about what we could and couldn't print. I'm just wondering why, after fifty years, there's still all this secrecy about what happened."

"The Archers were a very powerful family."

"Sure, they *were*, but they're not now. I don't think there are any Archers left in Crowford at all. Eric Grace and his lot pretty much crushed them. And that happened long before that piece we published, so why would Lou still be afraid of upsetting them?"

"You know Michael Archer died, right?" Julie asked.

Debbie nodded.

"It wasn't that long ago. There was a very brief mention of it in the Gazette, but I don't think Lou really wanted to go there at all. I think Michael was the last of the family, wasn't he? Isn't it weird to think that he died in poverty, a few miles from

Crowford, when just fifty years ago his family owned half the town? How the mighty have fallen, huh?"

"I heard that that's how Mr. Grace took over. When he learned about Michael's crimes, he basically blackmailed old Jonathan Archer. He took everything from him and left him in penury. Just imagine that, for a moment. You've built up a real little empire, and then one of your kids causes it to get completely trashed in the space of just a few years."

"Might I ask why you're so interested in this all of a sudden?"

"Just natural curiosity about a story I heard bits of while I was growing up," Debbie replied. "You know what? I think I might drop by and see old Lou later. Just for old times' sake."

***

"Wow," Debbie muttered an hour later, as she wandered across the office of the Crowford Gazette, "time really *has* stood still around here."

"I'll be out in a minute!" a familiar voice shouted from the back room.

Smiling at the thought of seeing Lou Faraday again, Debbie headed over to look at the far wall, where various important front pages had been framed and put on display. There were covers proclaiming the ends of wars, covers marking openings and closings of various buildings across the town, covers for local tragedies such as the Crowford Mill fire and the sinking of the Mercy Belle, covers for just about anything remarkable that had ever happened in the town. As she stopped and looked at one particular cover, from just a few years earlier, she saw her own name on the byline.

She smiled as she remembered how keen and eager she'd been as a young reporter. Even after Bradley had been born, she'd managed to work part-time, and then after her divorce from Dave she'd tried to throw herself back into journalism properly. Just as she'd been starting to gain some momentum, however, she'd noticed the first niggling pains that eventually turned out to be early symptoms of acute myeloid leukemia. Everything after that had been a blur.

"Can I help you?"

Turning, she saw Lou – looking so old now, with gray hair – emerging from the other part of the office.

"Wait," he said, adjusting his glasses for a moment, "Debbie Firth, is that you?"

"In the flesh."

"I was just thinking the other day, I should call your grandmother and see how you're doing!" He hurried over to give her a hug, but then he stopped at the last second. "Is it..."

"I'm fine," she said, taking the initiative and hugging him instead. "A little sore, and tired, but I'm getting about. And I'm certainly still capable of giving and receiving hugs.""

"And does this mean that you're -"

"In remission," she said as she took a step back from him. "It's touch and go, we won't know for a while which way things are really headed, but there's a chance. Still bald, though."

"You keep fighting, girl!" he said firmly. "And if you ever want to get back into the newspaper business, come and see me first, okay? Times are tight and sales are in the toilet, but I'm always ready to invest in quality reporters!"

"That's very kind of you," she said, as she headed over to the main desk and looked down at the next week's cover, which was already being put together. "Looks like things are humming along okay here."

"We get by," he said, shuffling over to one of the other tables. "Circulation is down by about a third in two years, advertisers think they should get twice the space for half the price, and now apparently every reporter thinks they have to have a mobile phone in order to get the job done. Oh, and I'm supposed to pay the bill! As you can imagine, my ulcer is bubbling away nicely."

"You've still got that thing?"

"It's never going away. It'll probably outlive

me."

He started shuffling through some papers on the table.

"Can I ask you a question?" Debbie said after a moment.

"Shoot."

She paused, fully aware that she might not get a very friendly reaction.

"Why did we cover up the identity of the man who killed those women?"

Lou turned to her.

"You know who I mean," she continued. "Michael Archer. He killed several women around the county and -"

"That's old news," he said, interrupting her. "No-one's interested."

"Are you kidding?" she replied. "Eve Marsh was killed right here in Crowford, and the other women were all killed within a few miles. People lap that sort of story up, and you're sitting on an exclusive." She waited for a reply. "You could double your sales overnight if you led on a front page splash revealing the truth. You could put a photo of the dead women alongside a photo of Michael Archer and -"

"Michael Archer was never arrested or charged."

"Everyone knows he killed those women. And everyone who was involved is long gone now, so who are you protecting? Even the Archer family is no more. There's not even a risk of getting sued anymore."

"You don't understand, Debbie."

"You're right, I don't, so explain it to me." Again she paused, and again Lou seemed lost for words. "Is it the police you're worried about? Obviously they were in on the cover-up too, but I'm sure everyone involved is at least retired by now. And sometimes journalism means ruffling a few feathers. Where's your campaigning spirit, Lou?"

"Crowford is a nice quiet town. It's not the kind of place where lurid murders are splashed across the front of the local paper."

"But this really happened!"

"What's it to you, anyway?" he asked with a sigh. "It's nice to see you, Debbie, but why have you suddenly got a bee in your bonnet about something that happened half a century ago? Not everything has to be a big news story, and not everything has to end up in the public domain. Something bad happened and it was dealt with, and no-one else got hurt. As for the man who allegedly was responsible, as far as I'm aware he spent most of his life living in abject poverty, alone and unloved, blamed for the downfall of his family. Is it fair that he didn't end up in a jail cell, and that the whole thing was basically resolved as part of a business transaction? Maybe not, but it's what happened, and I'm not in the business of publishing crusader journalism. Believe me, nobody would thank you for dredging up the past."

"I guess that's that, then," she said. "I'm sure you're not remotely motivated by the fact that the Graces could destroy the paper if they instructed all their tenants to stop advertising with you."

"What are you suggesting?"

"I'm suggesting that there's a story here and you're ignoring it."

"It's for the best to just leave the past alone," he told her. "I understand, you want to come racing out of hospital and get stuck into a meaty campaign, but Michael Archer is nobody's project. The man is dead, and I'm not going to run a load of stories about someone who can no longer defend himself."

"You think he *could* defend himself?"

"I think it's good to see you up and about, Debbie. Take some time to relax. After everything you've been through, you must be exhausted." He paused. "And forget about the Archer case, okay? There's no-one left who cares about uncovering the truth now. All that nasty business has been put to bed, once and for all."

CHAPTER SEVEN

"WHAT HAPPENED?" CHRISTIAN ASKED as he and the others hurried into the changing room. "What did you see?"

"I don't want to talk about it," Charles said, immediately turning away from them. He was wearing some ill-fitting clothes from the lost property box, having soiled his own.

"Did you see the ghost?" Simon asked. "Come on, you have to tell us!"

Hanging back a little, Bradley could see the severe discomfort in Charles' expression, and he felt a shiver as he realized that there was no way this discomfort was being faked. He'd known Charles for a long time, and he'd seen him carry out several pranks in the past, but this was clearly something different. Looking down, he saw that Charles' right hand was trembling.

"You ran out of there at full-speed," Simon said excitedly. "We heard you scream. What spooked you so much?"

"I said I don't want to talk about it!" Charles snapped angrily, keeping his back to them.

"What did she look like?" Simon asked.

"Did she come at you?" Christian added. "Did she *touch* you?"

"Maybe we should leave him alone for a bit," Bradley suggested. "Guys, if he doesn't want to talk, he doesn't want to talk. We have to be back in class in five minutes, anyway."

"Fine," Christian muttered, and he and Simon began to leave the room. "We'll get the truth out of you eventually, Charles. We want all the gross details!"

Hanging back, Bradley watched Charles for a moment. He knew he should follow his own advice and go with the others, but he couldn't shake the feeling that something was seriously wrong with Charles, something that meant he shouldn't be left alone. After a moment, he even thought that he could see tears in the other boy's eyes.

"Are you okay?" he asked finally. "Do you want me to fetch someone?"

"You don't believe me," Charles whimpered.

"You haven't really said anything yet," Bradley pointed out.

He waited, and he once again saw that Charles' hands were shaking. Torn between feeling he should leave and worrying that Charles needed company, he finally stepped a little closer.

"She was right there," Charles said cautiously, his voice tense with fear. He was staring into space, as if he couldn't get the image out of his head. "I saw her, man. I saw Eve Marsh, and I'm not even joking. She was looking right at me from the other end of a corridor, like she hated me, and I swear I could tell that she wanted me dead."

"Did she say anything?"

Charles hesitated, before shaking his head.

"She didn't really need to," Charles continued. "She'd written it on the walls, even on the windows. Everywhere."

"Written what?"

"A name. Adam."

"Adam was the name of her boyfriend, wasn't it?" Bradley replied. "That's why it's sometimes referred to as the Adam and Eve murder."

"She's written his name on every surface in there," Charles explained. "I could hear a scratching sound, like she was still doing it. Whatever happened, I think she's definitely not over it. I think she wants revenge."

"You don't know that for sure."

"You didn't see her!" Charles hissed. "She's

dead, and she was standing there and looking at me! I could see her as clearly as I'm seeing you right now!"

"Okay," Bradley said, "I'm sorry, I didn't mean to doubt you. It's just that it's kind of hard to get my head around. I know people have talked about the ghost before, but you're the first person I've ever met who's actually seen her." He paused, trying to think of something he could do or say to make Charles feel better. "So what do you think we can do?" he asked finally.

"*Do?*"

"If there's really a ghost in there, someone should do something, shouldn't they? We should tell an adult or -"

"I told Mr. Kepper," Charles said bitterly, through gritted teeth, "and he laughed at me. He told me I was stupid and that everyone was going to laugh at me for messing my pants and that I've got an overactive imagination. I hate him so much."

"I don't think *anyone* really likes Mr. Kepper," Bradley pointed out. "Not even Mrs. Kepper, if he's even married. I can't imagine who'd want to marry him, though. The point is, you shouldn't pay too much attention to what he says."

"Everyone's going to laugh at me," Charles muttered.

"No, they won't."

"Of course they will," he continued, and he

suddenly started rocking back and forth on the bench. "They'll be like Mr. Kepper, they'll say that I imagined it all and got confused. People don't believe it when other people talk about ghosts, not unless they've seen them themselves. Sometimes not even then. I'll be a laughing stock!"

Bradley opened his mouth to tell him not to worry, but at that moment the door swung open behind him and he turned to see that Mr. Kepper had stormed into the changing room.

"And what's going on here?" the teacher asked, putting his hands on his hips. "Charles, now that you've changed, you need to get back to the classroom. You're not going to get out of analyzing those specimens just because you had a little accident."

"Sir," Charles said cautiously, "I think -"

"Hiding away, are you?" Mr. Kepper asked with a grin. "Come on, boy, that's not how a man handles things. So you messed up. So what? You'll be better served by getting right back out there."

"Can I just have a minute, Sir?" Charles asked.

"I think he's really upset," Bradley added.

"Shut up!" Charles snapped.

"Sorry," Bradley murmured.

"You've had enough time to pull yourself together," Mr. Kepper said with another sigh. "You got yourself into this mess, Mr. Oliver, and now you need to learn to withstand life's slings and arrows. Believe me, there'll be plenty more of them as you get older. I don't know if anyone has told you boys about the facts of life, but let me promise you... Life is cruel and nasty, and mean, and you need to toughen up. Both of you."

Charles opened his mouth to say something, but he couldn't quite get the words out.

"Get out of here," Mr. Kepper continued, holding the door open for them. "Bradley, Charles, I mean it. Move. I won't have children hiding in the changing room all day."

Getting to his feet, Charles stormed out of the room, keeping his head bowed as if he was too embarrassed to let anyone see his face. Bradley hesitated, and then he began to follow.

"I don't want to hear any more stupid stories about ghosts," Mr. Kepper told him, as he took a pack of cigarettes from his pocket. "You're got a bit more of a level head on your shoulders than many of the boys in the class, Bradley. Do me a favor and try to dampen all this talk down, will you?"

"Yes, Sir."

"The last thing we need is to have all the kids worrying about ghosts," he continued, lighting the cigarette as he headed to the other door. "I'll be through in a minute, just tell everyone in the class to read until I'm there. I swear, this job is going to be the death of me."

Taking a long puff on his cigarette, he turned to Bradley.

"You know what'll be a good thing, Mr. Firth?" he added. "When they knock that old building down. The date's been brought forward, it's all coming down next week, and then a nice developer is going to build some lovely flats on the site. I've seen the brochure, I'm actually thinking of putting in for one of them. I reckon they could make nice little bachelor pads, if you catch my drift."

He took another drag on the cigarette.

"No, of course you don't," he added with a sigh. "Go back to the classroom, Bradley. Try to get everyone to calm down a bit."

He muttered something else under his breath, something inaudible.

Once Mr. Kepper had gone outside to smoke, Bradley turned and made his way out of the changing room. As soon as he was near the classroom, however, he realized he could hear raucous laughter, and a moment later he heard Charles desperately trying to get everyone to leave him alone.

"I don't want to talk about it!" he was shouting. "Stop laughing at me!"

A moment later, Charles stormed out of the classroom. His eyes were filled with tears and his face was bright red, and he didn't even notice Bradley. Hurrying into the bathroom, he seemed really upset, but Bradley figured that there was no point going after him. He could still hear everyone laughing in the classroom and mocking Charles, calling him all sorts of names, and he knew that sort of thing wouldn't stop for a while. Not until someone else did something to catch everyone's attention. In a strange sort of way, and for the first time in his life, Bradley actually felt a little sorry for Charles Oliver.

CHAPTER EIGHT

"OKAY," DEBBIE SAID AS she and Bradley sat on the sofa, watching evening TV, "you can finish this episode of *Dallas* with me, but then you're off to bed. Got it?"

"Can't I stay up a little longer?" he asked, snuggling closer to her. "It's your first night home."

"Just because I'm home, that doesn't mean that you get to sit up late on a school night," she told him. "When Nana went to stay at her house tonight, she specifically reminded me that I have to be tough on you. Now, are you sure you've got all your homework done?"

"I promise. Mr. Kepper didn't set us any for tonight."

"I can't believe you've still got that guy as your teacher," she muttered. "I went to school with

Roger Kepper."

"Is that his first name? Roger?"

She nodded.

"What was he like at school?"

"A complete and utter..." Her voice trailed off for a moment. "Never you mind," she continued. "He's your teacher, God help you, and you need to listen to him, and you also need to -"

Before she could finish, the phone began to ring in the hallway. Bradley instinctively began to get to his feet to go and answer, but Debbie put an arm on his hand to hold him back.

"Don't worry about it," she said.

"But what if it's -"

"It can't be anything important after eight," Debbie said, clearly a little uncomfortable. Scared, even. "If it *is* important, they can call back tomorrow, can't they?"

"But what if -"

"Just leave it, okay?" she added, a little more firmly than before. "I don't want any interruptions."

Bradley hesitated, before sitting back down.

"What if it's the same person who tried to ring during dinner?" he asked cautiously, as the phone continued to ring.

"Like I said, they can call back tomorrow if it's important." Debbie watched the door to the hallway with a growing sense of unease, until finally the phone fell silent. "There," she said with a relieved sigh, "now we can get back to watching *Dallas*. I'm really glad they're repeating these ones so soon, I missed all of them while I was in the hospital."

"Can I stay up and watch *Red Dwarf* later?"

"No."

"Please?"

He puts his hands together in mock prayer.

"It's really funny," he continued. "I think you'd like it too."

"Maybe," she said, rolling her eyes. "If you're good."

"I love you," he replied, wrapping his arms around her and giving her a big hug. "I'm so glad you're home. I hope you never have to go back into hospital."

"Me too," she said, forcing an unconvincing smile. "Now let's watch, okay? You have no idea how much I missed these simple evenings while I was in there. That's one of the reasons I told Nana it was really okay for her to go home tonight. I wanted it to be just you and me, like the old days."

She tousled the hair on top of his head, but after a moment her attention once again drifted away from the episode of *Dallas* that was playing on the TV. She looked toward the hallway again, and she felt a knot of fear in her stomach as she realized that the phone might ring again at any moment. And next time, she might be able to stop anyone answering.

***

Several streets away, in her semi-detached house on Clareforth Street, Josephine sat at her kitchen table and stared at the school photo that featured a smiling Eve Marsh. With tears in her eyes, Josephine seemed almost frozen by the sight, lost in her memories until she was suddenly startled by the sound of someone ringing the doorbell.

Getting to her feet, she hurried to the hallway and checked herself in the mirror, and then she pulled the door open and found herself face to face with Alan Walton.

"Good evening, Josephine," he said, with a slightly apprehensive tone to his voice. "I got your message, and I thought there was no time like the present to see what's up. So... what's up?"

"Please, come in," she said, gesturing for him to go into the hallway.

"I prefer to stay out here," he replied. "I really don't have long. Sheila and I have got the grandchildren for the week and I want to be home to put them to bed." He paused. "She said you sounded upset on the phone earlier. Is Debbie doing okay?"

"She's fine. Well, she's home from the

hospital on remission."

"That's fantastic news, Josephine! You should be focusing on this joyous miracle, rather than -"

"Why didn't you arrest Michael Archer?"

"Josephine..."

"I mean the real reason," she continued, still struggling to hold back tears. She took the tissue from her sleeve and dabbed at her eyes again. "I know the reason you gave me, the reason you gave everyone who asked, probably the same reason you told yourself. But you knew it was him, you knew he did all those awful things, and you let him stay a free man, even after his family had fallen from power in Crowford. I just want to know why."

Alan shifted uncomfortably for a moment, as if he was trying to come up with an answer that he just couldn't quite get right.

"Everyone knows what he did," she added. "Everyone who paid the slightest bit of attention, anyway."

"Michael Archer was only ever suspected of committing one crime in Crowford itself," he said finally, "and we have no evidence that he -"

"That's rot!" Josephine snapped. "How can you stand there and lie to me, to my face, like that? You were in charge of the investigation, Alan, and you know full well what that man was up to! I'm not just talking about what happened to poor Ms.

Marsh, I'm talking about all the other wretched things that he did!"

"I needed evidence, Josephine, and I didn't have any."

"You had enough to keep putting pressure on him, though," she said, as more tears filled her eyes. "What happened? Did old Mr. Archer force you to drop it?"

"Josephine..."

"I remember Jonathan Archer, you know," she continued. "Just about. He thought he was cock of the walk, didn't he? Michael's father thought he owned Crowford, and he more or less did. That's why, whenever anyone complains about Mr. Grace taking over, I always wonder what they'd think if they'd been around during the time of the Archer family's vice-like grip on the town. Because that's when the *really* bad things were happening in Crowford, isn't it? Michael was just the inevitable culmination of all that corruption and greed and violence that his father built up. He was a summation of the family, in a way. It seems somewhat poetic to me that he was also the reason why the Archer empire fell apart."

"With all due respect, I don't think you really know what you're talking about."

"And what about after the old man was dead? When was that, just after the war? Did he die of shame, once he saw the monster that his son had become? And then, eventually, Michael was all alone, he had no money and no power, and he still got away with..."

Her voice trailed off for a moment.

"You still *let* him get away with so much, for years. In fact, by my reckoning he only really stopped after you retired. Did he realize that your successor would never look away, the way *you* looked away?"

"I think it was a mistake for me to come here tonight, Josephine. You really don't know what you're talking about."

"Do you know what I thought when I heard that Michael died earlier this year?" she asked. "I thought it was the best news I'd heard in a long time. I'm a good woman, I'm a Christian woman, but I was so happy when I heard about that man's death. I know he spent his last years away from Crowford, living as a recluse in the middle of nowhere. I hope his death was slow and painful, and I hope that in his final moments he was visited by the ghosts of everyone whose lives were made a misery by his awful actions."

"I can't talk to you when you're like this," Alan muttered. "You're getting too emotional, Josephine."

"A woman died," she replied, as he turned and started walking away. "She was murdered, her body was defiled, and you let the perpetrator walk free." She waited for a response, but he didn't look back. "And because he was free," she continued, "he was able to do other vile things to people all across this county. Didn't you care, Alan? Don't you care now? Don't you ever look back at what happened and wonder whether you could have shown a little more backbone and prevented it?"

"Stop trying to dig up the past!" he called back to her.

"You can't dig up something that was never buried in the first place!" she shouted. "What about me? What about what he did to me?"

She watched as he rounded the corner and disappeared from view, and then she shut the door and stepped back. Sobbing now, she sank down onto the floor, still hopelessly dabbing the tissue against her eyes as more and more tears streamed down her face. She hadn't expected Alan Walton to admit to all his mistakes, not really; she knew he was a stubborn old man who preferred to ignore the past. At the same time, she'd hoped that he might at least acknowledge that he'd mishandled the case, that he might deign to admit that he could have done things differently. Instead, he'd simply repeated the same tired old excuses that he'd been trotting out for so many years.

"You let that monster roam free," she screamed, "and look what he did! Look what he did to us all! Look what he did to my family!"

CHAPTER NINE

"I'LL BE HOME SHORTLY, Sheila," Alan Walton said as he stood at the payphone in the back of the Crowford Farrier pub. "Everything's fine, I just stopped off for a drink with the boys on the way back. Come on, old thing, don't nag. Not tonight. Are Terry and Kayleigh in bed?"

He winced as she snapped at him, and then he heard her slam the phone down.

"And good evening to you too, my darling wife," he muttered, before hanging the receiver on the cradle and then collecting the extra coins that we spat back out into the little tray. He took a deep breath, and he hesitated for a moment before pushing the door open and going back through to the bar area.

"How did she take it?" Billy Simms asked

with a grin, as if he already knew the answer to his own question. "Sorry, I know Sheila's a lovely lady, but she never likes it when you go out drinking, does she?"

"She knows I always make it back safe enough," he said, before taking a sip of his pint. Cigarette smoke was swirling in the air all around them. "A little worse for wear sometimes," he added with a chuckle, "but safe enough."

"That'll be the ex-copper in you kicking in," Billy suggested. "No matter how soused you get, you've always got one eye on doing the proper thing. I suppose you just can't kick the training, can you?"

"Aye, and don't you forget that," Alan said, raising his glass. "Cheers!"

***

"Stupid bloody woman," he said to himself under his breath an hour later, as he stumbled home through the darkness of late-night Crowford. "Some people just don't know when to leave a thing be."

Reaching the crossing, he stopped for a moment to look at the empty roads, and then he shuffled over to the opposite pavement. There wasn't another soul in sight, and several minutes had passed since he'd last seen a car on the road. He'd walked the same route home from the pub hundreds – probably thousands of times – in the past, and he was approaching the part of that route that he liked the least. As he crossed another road, he glanced along a nearby alley and saw the dark shape of Crowford's old school building.

Stopping, he thought for a moment of the fact that he'd always avoided taking a shortcut across the school grounds. Going that way would save him a good fifteen minutes on his walk home, but he'd always taken the longer, more circuitous route. Now he was starting to think that he'd been foolish in the past, so finally he turned and made his way along the alley, telling himself that he was going to take some of his own advice for once.

The past was the past.

Sod anyone who said differently.

Once he was out of the alley, he began to shuffle across the old schoolyard. At first he told himself to just keep looking straight ahead as he made his way toward the new area of the school, but he soon found himself looking at the old building. He felt a little out of sorts, but also pleased with himself for finally taking the most logical route home. He had to admit, though, that he'd been glad to hear earlier in the day that the old building was being demolished in less than a week's time. It would feel good, he believed, to have some nice new flats put in its place. Something useful. Something modern. Something to put the past in the

-

Suddenly he stopped as he heard a distant, distinct bumping sound coming from over by the old building. He told himself that there was no reason to worry, but then he watched as the front doors slowly creaked open.

For a moment, Alan Walton simply stared at the open doorway, which in some strange way almost seemed to be inviting him to go inside. At the same time, he knew that there was no reason to be worried, and that obviously some damn fool had neglected to lock the doors properly.

He briefly considered setting off on his way again, but then he realized that it was his civic duty to ensure that the building was properly secured, so he began to wander over. He could feel a flicker of fear in his belly, but that was entirely overridden by his insistence on doing the right thing. Even as he made his way up the steps that led to the doorway, he was focused on the fact that he had to make sure that there was no funny business going on, and that no idiotic local children were causing trouble.

Stopping at the entrance, he looked through into the hallway.

In that moment, he remembered the day – fifty-two years earlier – when he, as a constable in the police force, had arrived with his colleagues and found the butchered corpse of Eve Marsh up in the school's main hall. He'd seen some shocking sights over the course of his police career, but the sheer horror of that day had always lingered in the back of his mind, and he felt a shudder pass through his chest as he thought of the poor girl's body, and of all the blood that had been sprayed across the floor and the walls.

"Rest in peace," he murmured, before reaching out to pull the doors shut.

And then, stopping again, he realized he could hear a faint scratching sound coming from somewhere in the hallway. He told himself that there was no need to worry, that the building was most likely riddled with rats and other vermin, but he also knew that any responsible man would go inside to double-check. A part of him was worried about setting foot in the school again, but he refused to be beholden to any kind of superstition, so he forced himself to step forward into the cold hallway and look around. There was just enough moonlight streaming through the windows for him to be able to see.

"Hello?" he called out, and his voice echoed in the empty space. "If anybody's here, you need to make yourself known right now, do you hear? I'm a former police officer and I won't have any messing about."

He waited, and after a moment he realized that the scratching sound was coming from one of the far corners, just beyond the bottom of the staircase. He hesitated, and then he made his way over to take a closer look, at which point he finally saw that the name Adam had been scratched into the wall hundreds, perhaps even thousands, of times.

"What in the..."

His voice trailed off as he looked up toward the top of the stairs. Even in the moonlight, he could just about tell that the name had also been scrawled across the surfaces up there. For a few seconds he stared in wonder, but then the scratching sound abruptly stopped. He began to turn, just as the sound returned, but this time it seemed to be coming from right in front of him.

And that's when he saw it.

To his horror, he watched as a thick scratch began to cut through one of the few bare patches of wall. Another scratch followed, then another, and Alan took a step back as he realized that some invisible force seemed to be scratching the name once again into the wood.

ADAM.

Telling himself that he had to be imagining things, Alan stood firm, but a moment later the scratching started again with another A, then another D, another A and another M.

Then again, a little further up.

And again, to the left.

That same name was being scratched into the wall right before him, each time with a little more force.

As the last line was added to the latest M, Alan finally turned and began to stumble toward the doorway. He'd seen enough, and he told himself that although he was most likely imagining things, he still didn't want to stick around and find out. Before he could get to the doors, however, they suddenly swung shut, slamming against the frame with force. He reached out and grabbed the handle, only to find that the doors were now stuck, and he began to panic as he realized that he was somehow trapped in the building.

"I won't have any fooling about, do you hear?" he called out, convinced that somebody had to be outside, holding the door shut. "You'll let me out of here at once, or you'll face the full consequences of the law!"

Although he was trying not to panic, Alan couldn't help but try the handles over and over, determined to get the doors open. And then, a moment later, he heard the sound of a footstep pressing firmly on a floorboard over his shoulder.

He froze, telling himself that he was alone, but he could already feel the hairs starting to stand up on the back of his neck. His hands, which had been gripping the door's handles, slowly slipped down, and after a moment's hesitation he turned and looked to see who was behind him.

Eve Marsh screamed as she reached out and

clamped her hands on either side of his head. Gasping, Alan tried to pull away, but blood was already running from his nose and a moment later his mouth began to froth as he dropped to his knees and let out one final agonized groan. His eyes were open wide with horror, reflecting Eve's hideous snarl as his pupils grew larger and larger.

CHAPTER TEN

"MUM? I CAN'T SLEEP."

Looking up from her papers, Debbie saw Bradley standing in the doorway, wearing his new red dressing gown. He was rubbing his eyes and he certainly looked sleepy, and in truth she'd been expecting him to put in a reappearance; after all, he hadn't seemed to keen to go to bed earlier, and she was pretty sure he was going to try to get out of going to school the following day.

"It's late," she told him, checking her watch and seeing that midnight was fast approaching. "You've got school tomorrow, remember?"

"But I can't sleep," he said again, shuffling into the room. "I don't know why. What are you doing?"

"I'm just looking at some very old things

from when I used to work for the local newspaper," she replied. "Do you remember when I was a journalist?"

He rubbed his eyes again, and then he nodded.

"It's just some really old stuff," she continued. "I shouldn't be sitting up so late, but..."

Her voice trailed off.

"Can't you sleep, either?" Bradley asked.

"Well, I haven't tried," she told him, "but no, I've got a funny feeling that I wouldn't have much luck." She paused, before using a foot to push out the chair on the opposite side of the table. "Come on, there's no point trying to force it if you really can't get to sleep. How about a glass of milk?"

"Can I have tomorrow off school?" he asked. "I don't think I'll be able to concentrate if I'm tired."

"Good try," she replied, getting up and heading to the fridge. "A nice glass of milk should help, and then you'll have to go back to bed."

"But -"

"And no arguments, young man."

***

The main doors of the old school building remained shut. Moonlight continued to fill the entrance hallway, where Alan Walton's bloodied body lay on the floor. His dead eyes were staring toward the foot of the stairs, and globs of thick saliva were caked around his mouth. He'd died screaming, filled with an intense pain that had made him feel – in his final moments – as if his mind was about to explode. Blood was still dribbling from one of his ears, causing a faint tapping sound as each drop fell against the bare wooden boards.

***

Debbie grabbed the milk bottle and began to pour a glass for her son, before turning and seeing that he was leaning over the table and looking at her papers.

"Actually," she said cautiously, "I'm not sure that you be -"

"Who's Michael Archer?" he asked.

"Sweetheart, you really don't need to know about that. You're too young."

She poured a second glass, and then she put the bottle away.

"This is to do with the Adam and Eve murder, isn't it?" He was kneeling on the chair now, to get a better view, and a moment later he turned one of the papers around. "I was right!"

"How do you know that's what it's called?" she asked, heading back over to join him and setting two glasses of milk down. She glanced at the papers, but there was nothing too horrific on display. Fortunately all the nasty stuff was buried at the bottom of the piles. "Ignore me," she continued as she sat down, "I just started looking into a few old stories from my days on the paper. It's your fault, really."

"*My* fault?"

"You're the one who started going on about ghosts at the old school." She slid one glass of milk toward him. "Even if bad things happened here once, you don't need to be scared. Crowford is a nice, safe place, and there's no reason to worry about nasty things."

"I'm not scared," he replied, "I'm just curious. Nana got really funny when I mentioned all of this."

"Your grandmother tends to go a bit loony sometimes," she replied, "especially when anything comes up about what happened at the school. You've got to remember, she lived through it. It's not just history for her."

"So why doesn't she want people to talk about it now?"

"Some people believe that the past should stay buried."

"Why?"

"Convenience, I suppose."

"But when does the past become the past? When's it so far back that it shouldn't be disturbed anymore?"

"That's an excellent question," she replied as she looked back down at the papers. "There are still plenty of people around who remember the Adam and Eve murder. They're all old, of course, but they remember. And for some reason, a lot of them seem to think that it should stay buried."

"What about Eve Marsh?"

"What about her?"

"What if..." He paused, worried that he might sound nuts. "What if *she's* still around?" he asked. "What if somehow she's still here?"

***

Slowly, a line was being sliced across Alan's dead cheek, then another, and another, forming the letter A. A moment later a new line appeared, forming the start of the letter D.

***

"Eve Marsh died a long time ago," Debbie said. "It's been more than fifty years."

"I know, but that's not what I mean." Bradley replied. "What if somehow... I don't know, I don't understand it completely, but what if *somehow* she's still here? Or still in the school. What if she doesn't want the truth to be buried?"

"Now you're straying into some pretty unusual territory," she said. "I think you should drink your milk and go back to bed."

As if to underline that point, she took a sip from her own glass.

"But what if her ghost *is* still in the building?" he asked.

"Bradley..."

"But what if it is? Wouldn't she want everyone to know the truth?"

"I... suppose she would," Debbie said cautiously. "I mean, everyone would want the truth to come out about something important."

"Like who murdered her?"

"This is a bit of a grown-up conversation for almost midnight on a Thursday night," she pointed out. "Bradley, I appreciate that you find this all very interesting, but -"

"Charles Oliver saw her ghost!"

"Charles Oliver? The boy who claimed he was abducted by aliens last year? The boy who stood up in assembly once and claimed, with a straight face, to have met a bog monster that lives in the forest? That boy has some imagination, I'll give him that."

"I saw him right after it happened, he was really upset and -"

"So this is the big gossip in the playground at the moment, is it? Ghosts and things that go bump in the night? And what'll it be next week? Vampires? Werewolves?"

"I just feel sorry for her," Bradley continued. "If she's in there, she's been waiting all this time for someone to find out who killed her. And now if the old school's going to get knocked down, what if time's running out? What if she's been waiting and waiting and waiting, always thinking that eventually *someone* would make sure that she got justice, and now the school's going to be destroyed and when that happens she won't have a chance anymore?"

"Why wouldn't she have a chance?"

"Because she won't have anywhere to haunt!" he pointed out. "I don't know, but if I was her, I think I'd be starting to get..."

His voice trailed off for a moment.

"To get *what*?" Debbie asked, with a hint of concern in her voice.

"Sad," he continued, and then a shiver ran through his bones. "Desperate. Like time's running out and I needed to do something to make sure people noticed me again. To make sure that what happened to me didn't get forgotten."

***

The first line was followed by another A, then an M, and then Eve Marsh's brief, agonized scream filled the entire building with such force that the front doors began to swing open, leaving Alan Walton's corpse visible from the yard, ready for someone to find it in the morning.

***

"Just close your eyes," Debbie said as she finished tucking Bradley into bed, "and you'll be out before you know it. Suddenly it'll be morning, and you'll have to get up for breakfast."

"Are you sure I have to go to school in the morning?"

"Yes. Now get some sleep."

"But I want to be with you!"

"We're going to go on a little trip on Saturday," she told him, "just you and me."

"Where to?"

"I don't know. I'll figure it out tomorrow."

Leaning down, she kissed him on the cheek, before turning and heading to the door. When she looked back into the room, she saw that Bradley had indeed closed his eyes, so she gently bumped the door shut before creeping downstairs. The last thing she wanted was to make even the slightest noise, in case that encouraged her son to get up again. By the time she got back down to the kitchen, she was actually starting to feel a little tired herself, although she figured she might as well stay up for a while longer.

Sitting at the table again, she started sorting through the papers until she found a newspaper clipping from a few years earlier, from when the Crowford Gazette had run an article covering the fiftieth anniversary of the Adam and Eve murder. She'd been slightly surprised that Lou had allowed the piece to go to press at all, given his general reluctance to get involved in the story, but eventually she'd understood: he'd been trying to settle the story once and for all, to use the article as a way of drawing a line under all the questions and emphasizing that no answers were ever going to come. It had been his way of adding a full stop to the case of Eve Marsh's murder.

And that felt wrong.

She took a sip of milk from her glass.

The more she looked through the old papers and articles, the more Debbie felt annoyed that Eve's murder was effectively being swept under the rug. Everyone knew who'd killed her, even if very few people were willing to say the words out loud. Although he'd lived the last years of his life in a state of utter destitution, Michael Archer had never had to pay for his crimes, he'd never been so much as questioned by the police. No journalist would touch the story, and no paper would print it. As far as Crowford was concerned, the truth could – and would – stay hidden forever.

Unless, she realized, someone forced them all to acknowledge what had happened. Someone, perhaps, with nothing to lose.

***

Up in the main hall of the old school building, every square inch of the walls and floor and ceiling had been covered in the name Adam, scratched into the wood and glass.

A shadowy figured dropped to its knees, put her head in her hands and – surrounded by so many markings – began to shake violently as she murmured one word over and over.

"Adam," she groaned. "Adam. Adam. Adam..."

CHAPTER ELEVEN

"MUM, WHAT'S GOING ON over there?"

As she was about to lead Bradley toward the school's main gate, Debbie turned and saw flashing blue lights over by the old building. She and Bradley stopped and watched for a moment, before being joined by a few other parents who'd noticed the same thing. Within another half minute, a small crowd had begun to gather.

"Do you know what's going on?" another mother asked. "Should we be worried?"

"I don't know," Debbie replied, using a hand to shield her eyes from the sun, and squinting as she tried to see exactly what was happening. She could just about make out an ambulance and a police car, and figured making their way in and out of the building. "Whatever it is, it must be serious."

"Maybe it's to do with the ghost of Eve Marsh," Bradley whispered.

Clearly unimpressed, Debbie turned and looked at him.

"Or not," he added with a shrug. "It might be a total coincidence."

***

"No way!" Simon gasped as he leaned across his desk in class. "A body?"

"We overheard it on our way in," Christian said, his voice filled with excitement. "They weren't letting anyone go through that end of the yard, and one of the policemen was talking about whether or not they could start to move a body. Someone died in the old school building last night!"

"We don't know that for sure," Bradley pointed out.

"You know it's true," Christian replied. "Now, I don't have any idea *who* died there, but isn't it obvious that the ghost of Eve Marsh must have been responsible? She appeared to Charles yesterday, and now she's killed someone. Who knows what she'll do next? She must be *really* evil!"

"Speaking of Charles, where is he?" Bradley asked, looking over at one of the other desks and spotting an empty chair. "He's normally here by now."

"Maybe he never recovered from yesterday," Christian said. "Maybe somehow Eve Marsh followed him home and killed him. Not that they'll admit that to us, of course. They'll try to cover it all up."

"I heard that he wasn't very well last night," Simon said cautiously.

"Did you phone him?"

"No, I just heard someone saying that he looked really pale and poorly when he was picked up, and then after he got home he just got worse and worse. That's not really a surprise, though, is it? I mean, if he saw an actual, real ghost, then he's probably all messed up. I wouldn't be surprised if he's gone completely mad. They might have to put him in an asylum for the rest of his life."

"He's probably just whining to get a day off," Bradley suggested.

"Or he's a goner," Simon replied. "Think about that for a moment. What if he's been driven mad by a ghost?"

"There you go!" Christian said triumphantly. "This is all starting to boil make sense! And now we know that the old school is going to get knocked down in about a week, so we don't have long."

"Long to do *what*?" Bradley asked cautiously.

"We talked about this before," he continued. "We need time to plan, so this weekend is too soon.

And now next weekend's not an option, so I propose that we go in there on Monday lunchtime."

"Into the old school?" Bradley replied. "Are you serious?"

"Deadly," Christian said, turning to him. "It's okay, you don't have to come if you're scared."

"I never said I was scared!"

"I won't tell anyone. Well, maybe just a few girls. What's the name of that girl you like in Miss Baker's class again? That's right, Annie Weaver. What if I tell her that you're terrified of the ghost?"

"I'm not scared!" Bradley hissed.

"Fine," Christian continued, "whatever. We'll keep it to just the core team, just the three of us. We'll plan it over the weekend, and we'll execute that plan on Monday. Lunchtime's really all we need, it won't take us a whole hour to go in and look around, not if we're streamlined."

"What if we get in trouble?" Simon asked.

"There's no place for fear on this team," Christian told him. "Step one, we need to take an inventory of any useful equipment that we should take into that place. We need to think outside the box here and really try to imagine anything at all that could come in handy. Step two, we need to draw up a plan of action so that we don't waste any time while we're in there. And step three, we need to make sure that when we *do* see the ghost of Eve Marsh, we're able to document what happens so we can prove it to other people."

"Okay," Bradley said, furrowing his brow, "but I still don't see how we're going to be ready to do all of this by Monday. That's three days away, it's not enough time to come up with a proper plan."

"We have no choice," Christian replied. "Who's in?"

"I suppose," Simon said, although he sounded a little reluctant.

"What about you?" Christian continued, turning to Bradley. "Are you coming with us, or are you going to be a little chicken?"

"I'm not a chicken!"

"Then what's your answer?"

"Fine," Bradley said, as he spotted Mr. Kepper entering the room, "but let's just keep it from anyone else, okay? This needs to be just the three of us."

"Agreed," Christian replied, "but we should probably have a name for our team."

"Do we *need* a name?" Bradley asked.

"The Crowford Busters!" Simon suggested excitedly.

"Everyone settle down, please," Mr. Kepper said as he opened the register.

"We'll think up a name over the weekend," Christian said, "but for now, you really need to think about what you can each bring to the mission. I want actual, deliverable skills, not fancy ideas that will have no practical value. This is going to be a life or death situation."

"Have you been watching war films again?" Simon asked.

"Boys, will you please sit down?" Mr. Kepper called out. "I won't ask you again."

"Simon, do you still have that disposable camera?" Christian asked.

"I've used a few shots, but there should be about twenty left. I don't have any money to get the film developed, though."

"We'll worry about that once we know we've got proof of the ghost on there," Christian said, "and -"

"SIT DOWN RIGHT NOW!" Mr. Kepper yelled, storming over to them with such force that the floor shuddered. He slammed a fist against Simon's desk. "What have I told you boys about talking during registration?"

"Sorry, Mr. Kepper," they all said, quickly returning to their seats.

"This isn't playtime!" he continued, with his voice still raised. Every time he shouted, he sprayed a thin mist of saliva from his mouth. "Do you want to be late for assembly?"

"No," Simon murmured.

"Then sit down, and shut up," Mr. Kepper said, before adjusting his tie as he headed back to his desk. "Sometimes I wonder what's wrong with some of you. It's not rocket science, you know. During registration and assembly, you keep your mouths shut unless you're spoken to! Sometimes I don't know whether I'm working in a school or a zoo."

"Sorry, Sir," Bradley said, as he glanced at Christian and Bradley.

Grinning, Christian gave him a quick thumbs up.

***

Ten minutes later, sitting cross-legged on the floor in assembly, at the back near the fold-out indoor climbing frame, the boys listened as their headmaster, Mr. Ripple, solemnly told them why they might see a lot of activity over by the old school building. He'd managed to avoid any details, but he'd made it very clear that something serious had occurred.

"Another thing I want you to promise me," he said, "is that you won't respond to any reporters who might try to get you to comment. There are some unscrupulous sorts around, and I wouldn't put it past one of them to have a go. So what are you not to do?"

"Talk to them," around half the children said, while the other half looked rather confused.

"I told you," Christian whispered to Bradley,

"something really gruesome must have happened over there. Someone *was* murdered!"

"We don't know that for sure," Bradley replied.

"I'm sure of it. In fact, I've never been so sure of anything in my whole life. The only question is *who's* dead, and what did Eve Marsh do to him? Or her, obviously."

"Then why do you want us to go in there on Monday?" Bradley asked. "Shouldn't this make us maybe change our plans?"

"Are you kidding? This makes it more important than ever that we get in, document the existence of Eve Marsh's ghost, and then take that proof to the world. Plus, if we find out what she wants, we might be able to help her."

"Quiet at the back there!" Mr. Ripple called out. "Now, everyone stand, and we shall sing hymn number eighteen, Black and White."

Not wanting to attract any more attention, Bradley joined the others in standing, and then he looked down at the hymn book in his hands. After a moment, however, he realized that Christian was staring at him. He tried to ignore him, but finally he looked over just as everyone began to sing.

Once again, Christian gave him a thumbs up, to which Bradley could only offer a faint smile.

CHAPTER TWELVE

"HONESTLY, WE WERE FINE," Debbie said as she put the iron away and then shut the door to the cupboard. Turning, she saw her mother putting some laundry into the machine. "It was just me and Bradley, watching TV and spending some time together. It's what I dreamed about, all those nights when I was in the hospital."

"I'm glad, dear," Josephine replied. "You need to rest."

"I need to *live*," Debbie said.

"When do you have to go to the hospital again?"

"A couple of weeks, for some tests."

"A couple of weeks? That seems like quite a long time away, dear."

"That's what they told me."

"Are you sure you shouldn't call them and check?"

"I'm pretty sure they know what they're doing," she said, struggling to hide the fact that she wasn't quite being honest. "Don't worry, I can keep track of what I need to do and when I need to do it. Anyway, what did *you* do last night?"

"Oh, nothing of interest," Josephine said. "I watched the news and a documentary, a few other things, and then I read for a while. The life of an old widow isn't really that exciting, you know."

"Why don't you stay tonight?" Debbie asked. "We could have a family night in."

"And miss the Fuchsia Society?" As she turned the machine on, Josephine seemed genuinely shocked by the suggestion. "Absolutely not. Sorry, dear, but we'll have to do something tomorrow evening instead."

"Sure," Debbie replied, "and -"

Before she could finish, the phone started ringing in the hallway.

"I'll get that," Josephine said, already hurrying to the door.

"No!" Debbie called out, but she was too late. She listened with a growing sense of horror as her mother answered the phone.

Please, she thought to herself, *don't be them. And it's them, you can't say anything about me.*

"Deborah? It's for you!"

The knot of fear tightened tenfold in an instant, but Debbie knew she had no choice now. She took a deep breath, and then she made her way through. Her mind was already racing as she tried to figure out how she could take a call from the hospital without letting her mother overhear; or, failing that, how she could ensure that the call didn't sound suspicious.

"It's that friend of yours," Josephine explained, holding the receiver out. "What's her name again? Jilly? Janey? Something like that. Janice?"

***

"Lou!" Debbie called out, hurrying along the street as she saw her former boss unlocking the door to the Gazette's office. "Wait!"

Spotting her, Lou immediately sighed. He turned back to the door and fiddled with the key, but he already knew that he wasn't going to get inside in time. That didn't stop him trying.

"I heard what happened," Debbie said, a little breathless as she reached him.

"I don't know what you're talking about."

"Cut the bull, Lou," she continued. "Julie called me. She still has some contacts at the police station, and apparently Alan Walton's the one who was found dead at the old school building this morning. You remember Alan, don't you? The guy who used to be in charge of the local police station?"

"I fail to see why that warrants you coming down here."

"Apparently his face was all cut up, with the name Adam carved into it."

She waited for him to say something, but he seemed almost frozen in place.

"Apparently," she added, "his body had been mutilated. According to Julie's source, it's been rushed off for an autopsy, but the police who arrived at the scene found that he'd suffered multiple injuries and blunt force traumas. Apparently his eyes were almost popping out of their sockets."

"I'm afraid I can't comment on hearsay and rumor," he replied, finally getting the door open and stepping inside, and then turning to her. "Debbie, I realize that this plays right into your hands, seeing as how you apparently want this story to become some lurid splash all over the papers, but I'd like you to consider the potential consequence of your actions."

"I'm sorry?"

"Alan Walton has a wife, and children, and grandchildren. Please, do you really think that they want to have nasty details about his death shared all over the place?"

CHAPTER THIRTEEN

"SO THIS IS WHAT we're going to do," Christian said as he sat cross-legged on the playground with Bradley and Simon. "Operation Ghosthunter -"

"Is that what we're calling it now?" Simon asked.

"I came up with the name during assembly this morning," Christian replied. "Don't worry about the name right now, that's not what's important. Anyway, Operation Ghosthunter begins at exactly midday on Monday, as soon as the bell rings for lunch. It's vital, and I mean *vital*, that nobody forgets their lunchbox."

"Why's it vital?" Simon said.

"Because we won't have time to stop for lunch, so we'll have to eat it on the go. Also, go to the toilet as soon as the break begins. I want to be out the door by five past twelve at the latest. All the teachers will be on the door of the lunch hall, which means all we have to do is go around the back of the special education hut and then sprint behind the bushes, and we should easily be at the old school building by ten past at the latest."

"And then what?"

"And then we go inside," he explained. "We make straight for the old hall up on the building's first floor, because that's where Eve Marsh's body was found fifty years ago. It stands to reason that the hall should be where her ghost is focused. Simon, you need to make sure that your disposable camera is ready to roll, and that the flash works properly."

"Should I use the flash if I'm taking a photo of a ghost?"

"Why wouldn't you?"

"If she's partly see-through, isn't there a risk that the flash will make it harder for her to appear in the picture? Or don't you think it'll make much difference?"

Christian thought solemnly about that question for a moment.

"Try both options," he said finally. "Flash on, and flash off. Hopefully you'll have the chance. Did you manage to think about how we can defend ourselves?"

"I've got some ideas," Simon replied. "I'll

work on them over the weekend, but I think I can get my hands on a secret weapon. I don't want to say too much right now, because I'm still not certain I can get into the boot of my dad's car, but I think I have a good chance. We should be ready to go on Monday."

"What about you?" Christian asked, turning to Bradley, who was looking across the grass, toward the distant old school building. "Hey, Bradley, are you even listening?"

Bradley looked over at him.

"Did you hear a word I just said?" Christian continued, rolling his eyes. "If Operation Ghosthunter is going to have any chance of changing the world, we all need to be utterly committed."

"I was just wondering whether we should be doing this at all," Bradley replied.

"Seriously?" Christian spluttered.

"Think about it," Bradley said. "What if there's no ghost? Then we're just wasting our time and risking getting into a whole heap of trouble. And if there *is* a ghost, then we're getting mixed up in something we really don't understand." He paused for a moment. "The building's getting knocked down in a week anyway. Call me crazy, but why don't we just... let it be?"

"We're standing on the brink of the greatest discovery in the history of mankind," Christian replied, his eyes wide open with shock, "and you're chickening out?"

"I'm not chickening out," Bradley said, "and I'll go there with you guys on Monday if you decide to stick with the plan. I just think that we need to be *really* careful about how we do this. If the ghost of Eve Marsh is in there, and if someone really died there this morning, then this could be a really dangerous situation." He waited for either Christian or Simon to agree with him. "What if she's angry?" he continued. "What if, now that the place is about to be demolished, she's desperate and she's going to start hurting people?"

"Those are all reasons why we have to go in there!" Christian said firmly. "Bradley, seriously, I'm starting to get worried about you. I'd have thought you'd want to know the truth about ghosts and prove that they're real." He paused for a moment. "I mean, you know," he added, "since your mum's basically dying of cancer."

"Christian!" Simon hissed.

"But don't you want to know that she can come back as a ghost?" Christian asked, keeping his eyes fixed on Bradley. "That way, her being dead won't even be that big of a deal. She can be your ghost mum, she'll probably be even cooler if she's a ghost. Think about it, you wouldn't have to worry, and neither would she. Dying would just be something that'd suck for a little bit, it'd be one bad day, and then she'd come back all transparent and floaty."

"She's not dying!" Bradley said angrily, with tears in his eyes.

"Then why does she still wear that turban? I saw her at the school gate this morning, and I'm telling you, she didn't look well. She was really pasty, and she had bags under her eyes, and to be honest she looked like she was going to fall over at any moment."

"You don't know what you're talking about," Bradley replied, "and for your information, she's been allowed home by the -"

Before he could finish, they all heard an anguished scream coming from somewhere over near the school's office. They hesitated, and then they got to their feet and hurried over as the scream continued. The two dinner-ladies were trying to get everyone to stay back, but they were having no luck. Whatever was happening, it seemed to be somewhere near the main entrance to the modern building, and a bunch of other children joined them as they made their way around the corner and saw – to their shock – that the scream was coming from Charles Oliver, who was desperately trying to wriggle free as his mother held onto him tight.

"I'm not going in there!" he shouted. "I'm not going back!"

"Come on, Charles," Mr. Ripple was saying,

trying to negotiate with the boy, "it's not so bad. Just give it a try."

"No!" he yelled. "I'm never going back there again! She could be anywhere!"

"Maybe we should try again tomorrow," Charles' mother said as she began to lead him back over to the car park. "This might have been a little too soon."

As soon as he could, Charles pulled away and raced toward the car.

"I'm sorry," Mrs. Oliver said to Mr. Ripple, as everyone watched. "I don't think this is one of his usual pranks, I think he's really scarred by whatever he thinks happened the other day. I know it's all in his head, but it feels really real to him. I'd better get after him, but we'll try again on Monday. Sorry again."

Quite a large crowd had gathered by now, and after a moment Mr. Ripple turned to them all.

"What are you doing here?" he shouted, causing them to immediately turn and hurry back around to the playground. "You're not allowed around this side, not during the day. Get back to the playground immediately!"

"Charles is seriously messed up," Simon pointed out.

"It's the ghost of Eve Marsh," Christian replied, as the three of them headed back across the playground. After a moment they stopped and looked at the old school building, which stood all alone on the far side of the main field. "Charles wasn't prepared when he went in there. He was like an innocent little lamb, heading in to be slaughtered. He's probably lucky to be alive, but we're going to be ready for whatever she throws at us."

"What if we end up like him?" Simon asked.

"We won't," Christian said firmly, before turning to Bradley. "I'm sorry about what I said about your mum earlier. If you don't want to do this, I understand, but you need to decide now so that Simon and I can change our plans. Are you in, or are you out?"

For a few seconds, Bradley simply stared at the distant building. He couldn't help thinking about Eve Marsh's ghostly figure, lost and abandoned and waiting for the truth about her murder to come out. The thought of actually seeing her was terrifying, but at the same time he could feel the lure of curiosity. Although he'd reacted badly to Christian's comments a few minutes earlier, he knew that they'd contained a glimmer of truth, and he also knew that he couldn't back down now, no matter how scared he might feel.

"I'm in," he said, turning to the others.

"You sure?" Christian asked.

"I'm going in there on Monday, even if you two don't," he said firmly, holding a hand out. "We're going to do this thing."

"Agreed," Christian replied, as he and Simon bumped his fist. "Operation Ghosthunter is going to be the biggest thing that's ever hit this town. By the time we're finished in there on Monday afternoon, Crowford – and the world – will never be the same again."

CHAPTER FOURTEEN

THE NEXT AFTERNOON, AS he and Debbie sat on a bench outside a pub in the nearby village of Crossley Morton, Bradley looked out across the village green and saw some men walking past dressed in old-fashioned clothing. They looked like they'd arrived from some other time hundreds of years earlier, and Bradley found them strangely fascinating as they crossed the main square.

"Mum," he said after a moment, "who are *they*?"

She followed his gaze and watched the men for a few seconds.

"Probably some kind of historical reenactment society," she suggested. "Crossley Morton's known for that kind of thing." She paused. "You know what this village is *really* famous for, don't you?"

He turned to her.

"Ghosts," she continued with a smile. "Crossley Morton claims to be the most haunted village in the whole country."

"Is that true?"

"Who knows?" she replied. "I'm sure there are a lot of other places that claim the same thing. The only story I really remember is something about a headless man who's supposed to haunt Crossley Manor. I remember a lot of people talking about that when I was younger. Oh, and I think there was a weeping woman at some wishing well. They say she drowned down there a few hundred years ago, and at night you can sometimes still hear her sobbing." She watched him for a moment. "Do you get scared when you hear stories like that?"

"No," he said, although he felt bad for lying. He simply wanted to seem brave. "If there really are ghosts," he continued, "then why hasn't someone managed to prove it yet?"

"That's the million dollar question, isn't it?" she said, as the man from the bar brought their food over. "Hungry?"

Bradley watched as the man set the plates down, but he was still thinking about the idea of ghosts. He couldn't stop worrying about Operation Ghosthunter, although he knew that he couldn't tell his mother about what he and the others were planning. No adults could find out, otherwise the whole thing would be off. Christian had kept insisting that they were going to change the world, but Bradley was starting to think that if it was that easy to change things and to prove that ghosts existed, someone would have done it before.

"If ghosts are real," he continued "shouldn't someone have managed to take a photo by now?"

"You'd think. And that, Bradley, is how we know that they *aren't* real."

"They might be!"

"No, sweetheart, they're not. Honestly."

He looked over his shoulder and watched as the strangely-dressed men disappeared into a side street.

"Come on, get stuck in," Debbie said, "or it's going to get cold. And then I was thinking we could go for a walk. You'd like that, Bradley, wouldn't you? Just you and me, going for a wander like in the old days. It'll be as if everything's normal again, at least for a few hours."

***

"That's the place," Debbie said later, as they wandered along a country path, past a field of sheep. She pointed toward a large building in the distance. "Remember I told you about Crossley Manor earlier? That's it."

"That's where there's a headless ghost?" Bradley replied, stopping for a moment.

"Well, in theory. That's what people say, anyway. But like I told you earlier, there's no such things as ghosts, except as scary stories to tell late at night."

Bradley squinted to get a better look. From where they were standing, Crossley Manor was little more than a dot on the horizon, but the entire scene seemed peaceful enough. Bradley found it hard to believe that there could possibly be some kind of horrible ghost in such a nice place, although after a few seconds he furrowed his brow as he realized that he might be jumping to conclusions.

"Why are ghosts always angry?" he asked.

"What do you mean?"

"In every ghost story," he continued, turning to her, "the ghosts are always angry about something. They're always scary, and they want to hurt people. Why?"

"I suppose they wouldn't be very good stories if the ghosts were friendly. Anyway, what about Caspar?"

"Caspar's a cartoon character," he pointed out. "I'm talking about ghosts in stories where you're supposed to think that the ghost might be real. Why are they always so upset about something?"

"I think that's the point of most ghost

stories," she told him. "Ghosts are supposed to be the souls of people who, instead of moving on to whatever comes next, stayed behind because they want revenge for something."

"Like being murdered?"

"Like being murdered."

"And then they go away once they've got their revenge?"

"I suppose they would, but in a lot of stories they just get stuck. Or maybe it's not something as simple as revenge, maybe it's more a sense of longing and sorrow, in which case can they ever truly be satisfied? I mean, did you ever see a *happy* ghost?" She stepped past him. "Let's keep going and try to reach the old -"

Suddenly her knees buckled, and she let out a gasp as she dropped down against the muddy ground. Rolling onto her side, startled by what had happened, she looked up and saw Bradley's horrified face staring down at her.

"It's okay," she said, already starting to sit up, "I'm just..."

Her voice trailed off as she realized her sight was becoming a little blurred. Reaching out, she grabbed one of the fence posts for support, but she could already feel some kind of inner heaviness pulling down inside her chest, as if invisible strings were attached to tiny hooks all through her body, and those strings were now getting dragged down toward the ground. She forced a smile, hoping to show Bradley that she was fine, but after a moment she had to grip the post more tightly as she realized that she was on the verge of losing consciousness. She'd had dizzy spells before, since leaving the hospital, but this was on a whole new level.

"Mum, are you alright?" Bradley asked, reaching out and touching her arm. "Mum, what's wrong, are you getting sicker?"

"No, I'm fine," she murmured, although now she could feel pinpricks of cold sweat all across her face. "Just give me a few seconds."

"Are you dizzy? Should I go and get help?"

"No. Just wait a moment."

She took a deep breath and tried to *be* fine, but deep down she already knew that the truth was catching up to her. The doctors had warned her that something like this would happen if she insisted on checking out of the hospital, and their predictions had turned out to be absolutely right. She'd only been home for a few days, and the initial euphoria of feeling normal was no longer masking the little hand grenades of illness that were going off throughout her body. Still, she'd found that the absolute worst moments only tended to last for a minute or two at a time, and she figured she'd be able to pull herself together for at least a little while longer.

One week.

That's all she'd wanted, when she'd left the hospital.

One normal week, maybe two, instead of constantly waiting to be told she was in remission and constantly getting disappointed. With each postponement of a trip home, she'd begun to feel less and less certain that she ever *would* get home. The fear had begun to eat away at her from the inside, until finally she'd made a decision that she'd known at the time was foolhardy.

"I'm okay," she said finally, as the very worst of the sickness began to fade. "I'm going to be fine."

Looking up at Bradley, she saw the terrified expression on his face and realized that the day out had perhaps been a terrible mistake, worse even than her decision to leave the hospital. Her plan all along had been to check back onto the ward after one week, or two at most, and go onto the chemo again. She knew the idea of checking out had been reckless and foolish, but she hadn't been able to help herself. She just wanted to spend time with her son. Now she was worried that she might traumatize him by getting sicker in front of him. Or worse.

"Are you really getting better?" he asked.

"Yeah," she lied. "Of course."

"You don't..."

His voice trailed off.

You don't look better.

She knew that was what he'd been about to say.

"I promise," she continued, although she hated herself for giving him false hope. "It's just been a long day, that's all. I suppose I might have been pushing myself a *little* hard since I got home. Why don't you help me up and we'll head back to the car?"

Bradley helped her to her feet, and she brushed herself down before they started slowly making their way back the way they'd come. Debbie had hoped to take her son all the way to the old war memorial in a field nearby, but now she had to admit that she'd been too weak to get him that far. Still, she figured that she could tell him about it, and that one day he'd be able to find it for himself. She just wouldn't be able to go with him.

CHAPTER FIFTEEN

THE BANGING SOUND WAS incessant, and Lou Faraday couldn't help but mutter a few choice expletives under his breath as he hurried through from the back office and headed to the door. His lunch break was sacrosanct, but the person knocking just wouldn't stop, so finally he pulled the bolt across and opened the door.

"What the hell do you want?" he spluttered, spraying sandwich crumbs from his mouth.

"I need to talk to you," Dr. Henry Lloyd said, clearly worried about something. He glanced around, to check that he wasn't being watched, and then he turned back to Lou. "It's important."

"So's my lunch," Lou replied, starting to push the door shut. "Come back another -"

"It's about Alan Walton's death," Henry said,

putting his foot in the way, to keep the door open. "Please, Lou, I don't know where else to go."

"How about anywhere else? I'm having my lunch!"

"I know, but you're the only person who might be able to help me," Henry continued. "I just finished performing the autopsy on poor Alan, and... Lou, I think the police want to cover up what really happened, and I don't know that I can let them do that. That's why I came to you. We have to expose the truth."

***

"What's in those folders?" Lou asked skeptically, as he backed against the desk and watched Henry set a pile of papers down.

"Photographs, mainly," Henry explained. "Reports, too. I had to be quick, but I managed to photocopy the documents before I handed them over to the investigating officer. Based on some conversations I had with him earlier, I'm absolutely convinced that he won't let any of this see the light of day."

"And where exactly do I come in?"

"The autopsy exposed some serious irregularities," Henry told him. "I wasn't able to pinpoint a cause of death, not exactly, but the poor bastard's heart certainly seems to have given out.

Unfortunately, he'd also lost a fair amount of blood, due to carvings on his -"

"I know," Lou said, interrupting him. "He had some cuts on his face."

"Not just any cuts," Henry replied. "They were in a very specific formation. They spelled out the name Adam over and over again, but before I even started the autopsy, I was informed in no uncertain terms that I mustn't include that detail in the report."

"Did they tell you why?"

"I don't think they thought they had to. Detective Sergeant Mellor simply told me that any surface injuries were not to be taken into account, and that I was to focus exclusively on determining the cause of death. It's perfectly obvious to me that he and the others don't want the true nature of Alan's death to become public knowledge."

"And what *is* the true nature of his death?" Lou asked, leaning back against the desk and crossing his arms.

"He was quite clearly murdered!"

"Says who?"

"Says the evidence I gathered!"

"I thought you said his heart gave out."

"The man's face is covered in scratches!"

"So? Couldn't he have done that to himself?"

"Did you know Alan Walton at all?"

"Of course I did. We had a good professional relationship, and I saw him at a few events over the years. He was a nice guy. A little fond of the booze, but that's not exactly a crime."

"He didn't scratch that name into his own face!"

"Okay, calm down," Lou said, "there's no need to get all dramatic about this."

"I have proof," Henry said, opening one of his folders and pulling out a range of photos, all of which showed various parts of Alan's body during the autopsy. "If people can see the truth, then it can't get covered up, not this time. Lou, you're the only person in town who can get this information out to everyone, that's why I came straight to you." He hurried across the room and held the photos out, forcing Lou to take them. "I know they're graphic, but you can censor the worst parts."

"I can't publish these," Lou replied, wincing as he saw a shot of Alan's bloated, bloodied face with the name Adam scratched into the forehead. "They're obscene."

"People need to be shocked if they're going to demand action," Henry suggested. "We can talk to Alan's family and warn them ahead of time not to look at the paper. Please, Lou, I need your help or Mellor and the others are going to just add this to the long list of crimes in this town that have been covered up. They want to rush out a statement claiming that Alan Walton died of a heart attack, but these photos clearly show that's not true!"

"The scratches could have been added after he was dead," Lou pointed out, still horrified as he flicked through the various images. "As I understand it, the body was just left out there on the floor for several hours before it was found. That's more than enough time for some yobs to show up and think it's funny to desecrate the corpse of a good man. Especially a man who upset quite a few of the local criminals over the years."

"We both know that's not what happened."

"Then what *did* happen?" Lou snapped. "Are you pushing ghost stories, Henry? Honestly, I thought you were smarter than that."

"I've never believed in ghosts in my life," Henry replied, "until..."

He paused, and then he hurried back over to the desk and pulled out another of the photos. His hands were trembling now, and as he turned back to Lou he seemed gripped by fear.

"Until *this*," he continued, with dread in his voice. "I discovered something else during the autopsy, Lou, something that disproves all your theories. Sure, you can claim that local yobs might have made those marks on Alan's face, but I know you can't explain this."

He held the folder out.

Lou hesitated, before snatching it and taking

a look. He stared at one particular photo, before closing the folder again.

"Henry," he said cautiously, "is that..."

"It's exactly what it looks like," Henry told him, "and it's impossible. Mellor wouldn't even consider it, he told me it had to be a hoax, but it's absolute cast iron proof that something very strange happened to Alan Walton." He paused again. "In fact, if you won't publish it, then I'll have to find someone else who will." He reached out to take the folder back. "The truth has to come out somehow."

"Hang on," Lou said, pulling the folder away so that Henry couldn't get hold of it. "Leave it with me, okay? This is obviously a sensitive situation, and I have a duty to look into the ramifications of publishing. There are rules about this sort of thing, and if I'm going to go out on a limb for you – and it still *is* a very big if – then I need to be absolutely sure of my legal and ethical position."

"I'm willing to swear in court that those photos are real."

"You might well have to," Lou told him. "Come back some time next week."

"We can't wait that long."

"Tough. If we're exposing this, then we have to do it properly. Come and see me in the week, and by then I should have been able to get in touch with a couple of people who can give me some advice. If these photos are real, and if they show what they appear to show, then this is a massive story and we can afford to take our time setting it up properly."

"Are you sure you're up for that, Lou?" Henry asked. "I don't remember the Crowford Gazette ever running any major stories like this before."

"Well, there's a first time for everything, isn't there?" Lou replied. "As a matter of fact, I was talking to someone about something like this only yesterday. I've been in the local paper business for almost forty years, and you're right, I've never handled a story that could go global. I guess that day might finally have arrived."

"I've never seen anything like this," Henry said. "I'm sorry for bursting in here so abruptly, Lou, but I genuinely didn't know where else to go. The idea of this all getting swept away is just..."

"You did the right thing," Lou replied, leading him toward the door, "and now you need to leave me to figure out the next part."

Opening the door, Henry stepped outside and then turned back to him.

"I think Alan would want the truth to be known, wouldn't he?"

"That's the kind of man Alan was," Lou said, before pausing for a moment. "And did you say that these are the only copies you have of these images?"

"I didn't have time to make any more."

"Then I'll take extra care of them," Lou replied. "Come back in a few days. Hopefully I'll have some good news for you."

He watched as Henry walked away, and then Lou locked the door again before making his way back over to the desk and taking another look at the photos. He hated the sight of Alan's body having been left in such a terrible state, so he quickly tidied the pictures back into their respective folders.

A few minutes later, out in the yard at the rear of the building, he watched as all the papers and photos burned to ash in a metal bucket.

CHAPTER SIXTEEN

"BE GOOD," DEBBIE SAID on Monday morning, as she stopped with Bradley at the school gate, "and I'll see you back here at twenty to four. Got it?"

"Got it, Mum," Bradley replied, as he spotted Christian and Simon arriving. He glanced at them for a moment, and then he looked up at his mother again. "Thanks for walking with me today."

"My pleasure," she replied.

Pausing for a moment, Bradley suddenly realized that this might be the last time his mother would walk him to school for a while.

"Do you have to go to the hospital this week?" he asked. "For tests, I mean."

"No," she replied, shaking her head. "Not this week. Next week."

"Oh." He hesitated, and then he realized that

it was time to go inside. "I'll see you later."

"See you later," she said with a smile. "Have a good day, sweetheart."

"Are you ready?" Christian asked as Bradley joined him and Simon on the walk toward the school's front door. "Operation Ghosthunter commences at twelve hundred hours, on the dot."

"Yeah, I'm ready," Bradley said, even though he really didn't like the idea of going anywhere near the old building. "I guess. But how are we going to get in there? I mean, the police are gone, but that place is always locked up and I don't think we should try to climb up to one of the windows."

"Leave that to me," Christian replied with a faint smile as they reached the door to their classroom. "I've had all weekend to come up with this plan. We're going to rely on good old-fashioned human incompetence."

***

"No, this is completely wrong," Mr. Kepper said with an exaggerated sigh as Christian stood next to him at the main desk. "How many times do I have to explain this to you? When you carry a number to a different column, you put it here, see?"

He made several notes on the page in red ink.

"You didn't read the information on the card very carefully, did you?" he continued, sounding supremely irritated. He stank of cigarettes and alcohol. "I'm going to walk you through it one more time," he explained, "and then you really need to make sure that it's drilled into your head."

"Sorry, Mr. Kepper," Christian said, as he slowly reached back and hooked the set of keys off the small table behind the desk.

As Mr. Kepper began to explain the multiplication system, Christian carefully separated the key to the old building from the rest of the set. He recognized the key easily enough, since it was old and rusty, and he soon had it in his pocket. He set the keys back down, and then he pretended once more to be focusing on his teacher's notes.

"So that's the one you've carried," Mr. Kepper pointed out. "That one, right there. Do you get it now? It's really not that complicated, Christian, I thought you had this figured out several weeks ago. Is your brain not quite switched on yet?"

***

"Charles isn't here again today," Simon whispered later, as he glanced over at an empty seat nearby. "I heard that he really *did* get taken away to an asylum this time, for real. Apparently he was wearing a straitjacket and he was screaming and trying to bite all the doctors as they took him out of his house on a trolley."

"He's probably just pretending to be poorly again," Bradley replied. "You know what he's like. Any excuse to stay home and watch TV."

"Not this time," Simon said. "His brain is completely destroyed."

"How does someone's brain get destroyed?" Bradley asked.

"It crumbled," Simon explained. "I don't know the details, but whatever he saw the other day, it was too much for his mind to handle. That can happen to minds sometimes, they can just break and then no-one knows how to put them back together again. In the case of James, I imagine it didn't even take much for him to break, because... Well, I guess we can all agree that James is a bit of an idiot sometimes."

"You've been watching scary movies with your brother again, haven't you?"

"Sure, for research." Simon glanced over his shoulder, to make sure that Mr. Kepper wasn't watching, and then he leaned back over to Bradley. "We have to watch out for ectoplasm."

"I don't think that's a real thing," Bradley said. "Ghosts aren't like... snails."

"It's totally a real thing! It's a sign that a ghost has been in the area. It's a kind of slimy green goo, although in some cases it can be a different color. I had some in a tub for a while, it might not have been real, I got it for Christmas but it ended up covered in dust and dog hair and battery acid."

Bradley and Christian both stared at him.

"The point is," he continued, "we have to be prepared for anything once we get in there. A man died in that building last week, and Charles is just a gibbering wreck chained up in an asylum somewhere. We're doing something really dangerous at lunchtime, guys, and we have to take it seriously. Or would you rather wimp out and just sit around making more plans for our comic?" He waited for an answer. "We're doing this for Charles. We're doing it to make up for what happened to him. To remember him, and to mark his legacy."

"For Charles," Christian said, holding out a hand, which Simon immediately shook.

"For Charles."

They both turned to Bradley.

"For Charles," he said, a little reluctantly, as he shook their hands. "By the way, you know there isn't actually an asylum in Crowford, right?"

***

"Okay, everyone to the dinner hall!" Mr. Kepper said as the lunch bell rang out. "You know the drill, ladies and gentlemen. I'll see you back here in precisely seventy minutes for a scintillating afternoon of geography. Try not to explode with excitement! We'll be talking about sediment a lot!"

"Move," Christian whispered, pushing Bradley and Simon out the door so that they could turn left instead of right, heading away from the dining hall.

"We're so going to get spotted," Bradley muttered under his breath.

"We're so not," Christian replied, before holding a hand up for them to stop as they reached the double doors that led to the playground. "Mrs. Purnell and Mrs. Warner are the dinner-ladies today. I guarantee you that they're going to walk past in about five or -"

Before he could finish, the two women ambled the door and headed around to the rear of the kitchen area. They were chatting to one another, and neither of them glanced through the window and saw the boys. After a few more seconds, they were gone.

"Told you!" Christian said with a grin, before leading Bradley and Simon through the doors and out to the yard. "I was studying their routines toward the end of last week, and it turns out that they're all really predictable. Let's roll!"

They quickly made their way behind the special education hut, keeping low, and then they hurried around to the hut's far end, where a large set of bushes provided perfect cover for the final part of their journey over to the old school building. The three boys glanced back to make sure that nobody was watching, and then they scampered across the grass and rushed toward the building itself. They were each carrying a backpack and a lunchbox, which made it somewhat difficult for them to remain inconspicuous, but finally they reached the wall next to the door and they ducked down.

"We're here!" Christian said, a little breathlessly. "I told you we'd make it!" He checked his watch. "It's only three minutes past twelve. We're ahead of schedule!"

"I've got a bad feeling about this," Bradley whispered.

"No, you haven't," Christian replied. "You're confident, like me. And like Simon. We stand on the brink of a monumental breakthrough in human understanding. Once we emerge from this place with proof of the existence of ghosts, mankind will have to rethink its understanding of... everything! I didn't want to say this earlier, because I didn't want to get anyone too excited, but I think we're on the verge of becoming the most famous people in the whole world!"

"I've got my disposable camera," Simon said, reaching into his backpack and pulling the camera out to show them. "And this."

He pulled out a salt shaker.

"It might help to protect us," he explained.

Next, he pulled out a bottle of water.

"I blessed this," he continued. "I think. I prayed over it, at least. That should do the trick, right?"

"It's worth a shot," Christian replied.

"And then there's -"

"We're wasting time here," Christian added, before Simon could pull anything else out of his backpack. "It's now five past twelve," he added, holding up the key he'd swiped earlier from Mr. Kepper. "Enough talk. Enough planning. Simon, Bradley, it's time for us to get to work. We're going inside, and we're going to find the ghost of Eve Marsh."

CHAPTER SEVENTEEN

STANDING IN THE DOORWAY, the three boys looked around at the bare, abandoned entrance area of the old school. The air was noticeably colder than outside, and the only light came through a few dirty windows high up near the tops of the walls. The lower windows had all been boarded up, allowing light to enter only through gaps at the edges of the boards. Over the years, leaves and other dirt had blown inside and were now piled in one of the corners.

"Flashlight," Christian said, before turning to Simon.

He waited.

"Flashlight," he said again, holding his hand out.

"I didn't bring one," Simon stammered. "I

thought, I mean..."

His voice trailed off.

"You brought a saltshaker and some dodgy holy water to a haunted house, but not a flashlight?" Christian replied.

"It was a genuine oversight."

"Well, we're not turning back now," Christian said, taking a deep breath before stepping over to the foot of the stairs. He looked up toward the landing. "We have to go this way. The main hall, where Eve Marsh was murdered, is up there."

"That's not where Charles said he saw the ghost, though," Simon pointed out, stopping next to him and turning to look along the corridor that led to a bathroom at the far end. "I think it was down there."

"The main hall is going to be more significant to her," Christian said. "We have to use our time wisely. Trust me."

"But -"

"I'm not taking suggestions from the guy who forgot a flashlight," Christian added. "Sorry, I know that's harsh, but it's also kind of true."

They both turned to Bradley, who had been lingering quietly in the doorway.

"Are you coming?" Christian asked.

"Sure," Bradley said, stepping forward.

"Don't forget to shut the doors," Christian reminded him. "There's no point advertising to anyone else that we're here."

Bradley pushed the creaking doors shut, before turning and making his way over to join the others. He looked toward the corridor, and he couldn't help but remember that Charles had claimed to see a ghostly figure at the far end. He watched the space where the ghostly figure must have been standing, but to his immense relief he saw no sign of anyone. Still, his heart was beating fast and after a moment he noticed all the scratches on the walls.

"Adam," he whispered, seeing the same name over and over again. A shiver ran through his bones. "Who did all this?"

"Who do you think?" Christian replied with a smile. "The ghost did it."

"Is that blood?" Simon asked.

They all turned and looked at several dark patches on the floorboards, over near the door where Alan Walton had died a few days earlier. They had no way of knowing that this was indeed the exact spot where the body had been found, but after a few seconds they turned to one another as if some deep sense of unspoken unease had begun to settle in each of their hearts.

"I'll go first, then," Christian said, finally starting to make his way up the stairs, which creaked beneath his feet. "Remember, guys, we've only got an hour. Even less by now."

Bradley and Simon glanced at one another, and then Simon was the first to follow Christian. Bradley hesitated a moment longer, before suddenly turning and looking along the corridor as he heard a distant shuffling sound.

He waited, holding his breath, but there was no sign of anyone.

"Hurry up!" Christian called down to him.

Figuring that there was safety in numbers, Bradley hurried after his friends, quickly joining them on the landing. Several corridors ran off in different directions, but Christian had already begun to edge cautiously along the darkest route.

"Is it me," Simon said, shivering slightly, "or is it *really* cold in here?"

"I can't believe you didn't bring a flashlight," Christian muttered. "That's the one thing that I thought was too obvious to even remind you about!"

"I don't like this," Simon told Bradley. "I know I might sound crazy, but I've got this really weird feeling that we're not alone here."

"Me too," Bradley replied, "and -"

Before he could finish, they both spun around as they heard the sound of a door creaking someone nearby. They waited, but there was no hint of movement, and a moment later they looked the other way and saw that Christian was already disappearing into the gloom ahead. They started to follow him, passing several open doors that led into dark, abandoned classrooms. Both boys continually looked over their shoulders, as if they were worried about a ghostly figure coming up behind them, but finally they caught up to Christian just as he pushed open a set of double doors.

"This is it," he told them. "This is the main hall, where Eve Marsh actually died."

Light was streaming through several tall windows on either side of the room, catching plumes of dust that drifted slowly through the air. The walls were covered in portraits of headmasters and governors of the past, and lists of former pupils, although every surface had been marked by the named Adam, which had been scratched into even the highest points. At the far end of the hall, a lectern stood on a stage area, on either side of which there hung tall, drab curtains.

"Does anyone else feel seriously creeped out?" Christian asked as he stepped over to the middle of the room and looked all around. "There are major vibes in here. Even if I didn't know that someone had been murdered here, I'm pretty sure I'd have sensed it."

"No kidding," Simon replied. "Do you want me to sprinkle some salt and holy water around, just in case? You know... as a precaution?"

"Better not waste it," Christian said, turning to him. "We might need that stuff later."

"Do you think she's really been trapped here, all this time?" Bradley asked. "It's been more than fifty years since she died. Has she been just wandering around in this empty place, all alone, with nothing to do except scratch her name into the walls? Wouldn't she..."

His voice trailed off.

"Lose her mind?" Christian suggested. "Anyone would. Why would dead people by any different?"

"So..." Simon hesitated. "Should we try to contact her?"

Bradley turned to him.

"We came all this way," he pointed out, "and so far she hasn't really shown any sign that she's here. We've heard one weird noise, that's all, and even that wasn't necessarily her. It might have been a squirrel or something."

"He's right," Christian said. "We can't waste this opportunity. We all feel her presence, so she must know that we're here. I suppose the fact that there are three of us might be making her nervous, because she's outnumbered."

"We're not splitting up!" Simon replied. "No way!"

"Relax, I wasn't going to suggest that," Christian told him, "I just meant -"

Hearing a brief, clear bumping sound – like a footstep – they turned and looked back toward the open doorway. They couldn't see anyone out in the corridor, but the sound had been distinct and all three of them knew that they couldn't just dismiss it as nothing. After a moment, however, they looked up and saw a balcony area overlooking the main hall.

"Up there," Christian said, squinting but still unable to actually see anything *on* the balcony. "There's where it came from."

"That must be the way up," Bradley said, nodding toward an open door in the corner, on the other side of which there stood a narrow, winding staircase.

"Why would the ghost be waiting up there for us?" Simon asked. "It's not like -"

Before he could finish, they heard another bump, and this time there was no doubt that the sound had come from up on the balcony.

"It might just be a good place to watch us from," Christian suggested. "Either way, we have to go and take a look."

"What if it's a trap?" Bradley said.

"It's twenty past twelve," Christian replied. "We're a third of the way through already, and we have nothing! Do you really want to get to the end of this, and have no proof, and have to live with the knowledge that we wimped out of going all the way?"

"No," Bradley murmured.

"If you two are too scared, then that's your choice," Christian continued, striding toward the open door, "but I'm not backing down now. I'll see you up there." Stopping at the door, he turned to them. "If you dare."

With that, he disappeared up the staircase.

"Do we really have to do this?" Simon asked.

"We'll never hear the end of it if we don't," Bradley said, before setting off after Christian. "Come on, you know how it is. Besides, he's right. We came this far, we might as well finish the job."

"I might just wait down here," Simon said meekly. "You know, to keep an eye out."

"Whatever," Bradley replied as he began to climb the stairs. He was so cold now, he was almost shivering. By the time he got to the top and saw Christian exploring the balcony, he couldn't help but hope that the next forty minutes would pass quickly.

He looked around, but the balcony was empty and there was certainly no sign of a ghost. Wandering over to the edge, he leaned on the railing and looked down to see Simon far below. As he did so, he felt the wooden floor creak beneath his feet.

"Anything?" Simon asked.

"Nothing," Bradley replied. From his new, higher vantage point, he had a better view of the entire hall, but this only served to confirm that there was no sign of the ghost. "We heard her up here twice, though," he continued. "It's almost like it was some kind of -"

Suddenly, before he could get another word out, he heard Christian scream.

AMY CROSS

CHAPTER EIGHTEEN

"I'VE GOT YOU!" Bradley yelled, rushing across the balcony as he saw the floor giving way and Christian tumbling through the gap. "Wait!"

Throwing himself down at the edge of the hole, he managed to grab hold of Christian's left hand, just about keeping him from falling ten feet down to the hall's hard floor below.

"Help me!" Christian gasped, dangling precariously and already starting to slip again. "Bradley!"

"I'm going to try to pull you up!" Bradley said, reaching down and grabbing Christian's arm. "You're going to have to help, though! I can't do it on my own!"

"I can't hold on!"

"The floor just fell away!" Simon shouted

from down in the hall.

"We know that!" Christian snapped as he tried in vain to pull himself up. "I'm not going to make it!"

"I won't let you fall," Bradley told him, although he was running out of ideas and he wasn't sure how to haul his friend up. "Just give me a moment to figure it out."

"I don't have a moment!" Christian shouted, straining every sinew in his body as he tried yet again to climb back up through the hole. "Bradley, help me!"

"Should I come up?" Simon asked.

"I'm going to count to three," Bradley said, struggling to hold onto Christian, "and then I'm going to pull as hard as I can, and at the same time you have to do everything you can to climb. Got it?"

"Hurry!" Christian yelled.

"One," Bradley said, preparing for the effort. "Two. Three!"

In that instant, he summoned all his strength and began to haul Christian up. Christian, for his part, was trying to reach up and grab the edge of the hole, although he quickly felt splinters slicing into his hand. His legs were dangling wildly, but after a moment he finally began to rise up through the hole.

"Nearly there!" Bradley hissed through clenched teeth. "You're -"

Suddenly his grip slipped, and Christian's sweaty hands fell away. Crying out, Christian plummeted from the hole, only to land with a thud on top of Simon, who'd been loitering directly beneath and trying to find a way to help. The two boys collapsed together onto the floor, both letting out pained grunts, and Bradley could only stare down through the hole and wait to see whether or not they were okay.

Groaning, Christian was the first to sit up, following a few seconds later by Simon.

"Are you alright?" Bradley called out to them. "Guys! Did you break anything?"

"You landed on me!" Simon said angrily, rubbing his head. "You could have killed me!"

"You dropped me!" Christian yelled.

Sighing, Bradley realized that they both seemed to be in more or less one piece. He began to sit up, before suddenly feeling an icy sensation against the back of his neck. In that moment, he remembered that he was now all alone on the balcony. He could hear Christian and Simon grumbling to one another down in the main hall, but the hairs on the back of his neck were starting to stand up and a moment later he heard one of the nearby floorboards beginning to let out a long, slow creak.

He told himself that he was just imagining things, but then he heard another floorboard move slightly.

Closer, this time.

"Bradley!" Christian shouted from below. "Are you coming down?"

Bradley opened his mouth to reply, but his lips were dry and he couldn't get any words out. Somehow, he knew that there was someone right behind him, and sure enough a fraction of a second later he heard a faint, guttural gasping sound. He began to turn and look, trying to force himself to be brave, but it took a moment before he was finally able to turn all the way.

He felt a rush of relief as he saw that there was nobody behind him.

Suddenly something bumped against his arm. Startled, he let out a cry as he scrambled past the hole and ducked into the corner. Turning, he looked back across the balcony and, although at first he saw nothing, after a couple of seconds he realized that one patch of darkness was noticeably darker than all the others, and he saw that this particular patch was roughly formed in the shape of a person.

"Bradley!" Christian yelled again. "What are you doing up there? We need to check out the rest of the building!"

Again he tried to reply, and again Bradley was unable to find the words. He blinked, and in that instant he realized he could just about make out a figure standing over on the far side of the balcony, staring at him. He blinked again and the figure became a little clearer; now he could see that she was a woman, older than him but still fairly young, and she was wearing a white and red dress. As the woman's dead eyes remained fixed on him, Bradley realized that she could only be one person.

"Eve Marsh," he stammered.

"Bradley!" Christian called out. "Seriously, get your ass down here! We don't have time for any more messing about!"

"Eve Marsh!" he replied, managing to raise his trembling voice a little. "She... I... I see her!"

"What are you talking about?" Christian asked. "You'd better not be trying to have us on!"

Bradley opened his mouth to reply, but no words came out. All he could do was stare at Eve, as she in turn stared back at him. He could feel the freezing air against his face, as if the iciness of the dead woman was somehow radiating out across the balcony. Looking over at the door, Bradley knew that he had to try to get away, but he couldn't bring himself to try; the ghost of Eve Marsh had so far not made a move toward him, and he was terrified that trying to run would only incur her wrath. Even as he heard Christian and Simon still shouting at him, he remained frozen in place and he felt sheer cold drips of fear slowly filling his heart. Even when, finally, he tried to at least get to his feet, he found he could do no more than scratch his fingertips against the floorboards.

"Please," he whispered, hoping against hope that the ghost would be able to hear him, and that she'd just go away, "don't hurt me."

He waited, and in that moment he realized that she seemed to have moved a little closer. He hadn't seen her take a step forward, but she'd somehow shifted in the air.

"What do you..."

His voice trailed off for a moment as he saw the sadness in her eyes.

"What do you want?" he asked finally. "If you tell me, maybe I can..."

Again, he found himself unable to finish the sentence. Before he had a chance to continue, however, he saw that Eve's mouth was opening slightly, as if she was on the verge of answering.

"Adam," she said softly, her voice cracking with fear.

"Adam?" he replied, looking around at that name scratched on the walls, before turning to her again. "You mean... the man who killed you?"

"Adam!" she screamed suddenly, lunging at him. "ADAM!"

"No!" he yelled, holding his hands up to protect his face, but at the last second he heard voices and footsteps racing onto the balcony.

"Now!" Christian shouted, rushing forward

and grabbing Bradley's arm, pulling him out of the way.

Stumbling, almost tripping, Bradley slammed against the opposite wall before turning to see that Eve's ghost was rushing at him again.

"Adam!" she snarled.

Suddenly a roaring sound filled the air, and Bradley and Christian both turned to see that Simon had stepped up behind the ghost and was holding some kind of portable device out toward her.

Eve turned to look at Simon.

"What's that?" Christian yelled.

"It's a Dustbuster!" Simon shouted at him.

"A *what*?" Bradley replied.

"A Dustbuster!" Simon said, as he tried waving the machine up and down in the air, still aiming it at the ghost. "You use it to pick up small patches of dirt! My dad keeps one in his car!"

"We know what a Dustbuster is, you idiot!" Christian told him. "He meant, what are you doing with it now?"

"Trying to trap her," Simon stammered, as Eve's ghost stared at him with a strangely blank expression. "It's on the highest setting, I don't think it's going to work!"

"Move!" Bradley yelled, grabbing Christian and Simon and forcing them toward the stairs. The Dustbuster, still running, tumbled to the floor in the process. "We have to get out of here!"

Racing back down into the main hall, the boys hurried to the double doors, only to find that they were shut. When they tried to pull the doors open, they discovered that something was holding them firmly in place.

"It's locked!" Simon shouted, unable to hide his sense of panic. "We're locked in! We're going to die! She's going to rip us to shreds!"

"Help!" Christian yelled, banging his fists on the doors. "Somebody help us! The ghost of Eve Marsh has trapped us and she's coming to kill us!"

Bradley looked back toward the door that led to the stairs, but so far there was no sign of the ghostly figure. Still, he had no doubt that she'd appear soon, so he turned and joined the other two boys in banging on the doors in a desperate attempt to either break them down or alert someone to their predicament.

"Help!" they all screamed. "Somebody -"

Suddenly the doors swung open. Bradley, Christian and Simon fell through, landing hard in the corridor, and then they looked up and saw a figure towering above them.

"What the bloody hell do you three idiots think you're doing?" Mr. Kepper asked, putting his hands on his hips. "Do you have any idea how much trouble you're in?"

CHAPTER NINETEEN

"AND THIS," MR. RIPPLE said, peering at the Dustbuster on his desk, "was... I don't follow. Were you planning to tidy up a little while you were in there?"

"That was for trapping the ghost," Simon replied, struggling to hold back tears.

"Why did you think *that* was going to trap her?" Christian asked, turning to him.

"I don't know," he whimpered. "I just thought it might be useful. I thought if we could suck her in there, she wouldn't be able to get out and we'd be able to take her to show people."

"How would she fit in that thing?" Christian replied. "She's too big."

"I thought that if she's a ghost, she might be like a kind of gas."

"Ghosts aren't made of gas," Christian said, before furrowing his brow. "Are they?"

"Is it broken?" Simon whimpered. "My dad's going to be so angry if I broke it."

"You boys are unbelievable," Mr. Kepper said, shaking his head. He was standing with his arms folded across his chest as he leaned against the wall. "I've got to admit, you should probably get points for creativity. At least that's one positive to come out of this mess."

"The fact that this whole farrago was quite obviously planned," Mr. Ripple continued, "only makes it that much worse, I'm afraid. It would be one thing if you three had simply decided on a whim to give in to your curiosity, but you clearly spent some time coming up with a rather elaborate scheme."

"And stealing my key," Mr. Kepper said. "Don't forget that part."

"I have not forgotten that part," Mr. Ripple said sternly. "I take a very dim view of theft."

"It was only when Kelly Williams told me that she'd seen Christian take the key," Mr. Kepper continued, "that I realized something was afoot. And then Darren Clarke said he'd seen these three miscreants sneaking off behind the hut as soon as lunch break began. Once I had that information, it wasn't difficult to piece together an outline of what was afoot. You have to get up pretty early in the morning to sneak something past me, young men."

"Quite," Mr. Ripple muttered. "The question now is, how do we ensure that nothing like this ever happens again? Not only did you put yourselves in danger, gentlemen, but you also caused significant damage to school property."

"It's going to get knocked down next week anyway," Christian pointed out.

"That's not the point!" Mr. Kepper shouted, before sighing. "That's absolutely not the point, and you know it."

"You boys could have been very seriously hurt," Mr. Ripple pointed out. "Or worse."

Simon finally started crying. His face was red and flushed, and tears dripped from his eyes as he lowered his head in shame.

"Blubbing won't help," Mr. Kepper added, before taking a tissue from the desk and handing it to him. "You three have only got yourselves to blame for all this nonsense. Go on, wipe your eyes. No-one likes a crybaby."

"And why were you in there in the first place?" Mr. Ripple asked. "What could possibly be of such interest in an old, rundown building that's been out of use for so long?"

The boys stood in silence for a moment, before Bradley realized that one of them had to answer.

"The ghost," he said cautiously.

"I beg your pardon?"

"The ghost," he said again. "That's what we were there for. We wanted to get proof that Eve Marsh's ghost is in the old school. We saw her, but we didn't manage to get proof."

"Simon dropped his camera," Christian said, clearly unimpressed, "but we got proof that there's really a ghost there! I swear we did!"

Mr. Ripple rolled his eyes, and Mr. Kepper sighed.

"We did!" Christian snapped.

"Where?" Mr. Kepper asked. "Where is this magical proof?"

"We lost it," Christian replied. "What I mean is, we were right on the verge of it, and we'd have had it if we'd just..."

His voice trailed off, and after a moment he looked over at Simon, who continued to cry.

"We'd have had it if our equipment man had just done his job properly," he added. "Sorry, Simon, but it's true. You really let the side down. If you'd managed to get one photo, just one, we'd be heroes right now."

"That's rich," Mr. Kepper said, rolling his eyes.

Before Mr. Ripple could say anything, the phone on his desk began to rang. He answered and listened to a message, and then he set the receiver back down.

"Well, boys," he said, "you will probably not be particularly thrilled to learn that your parents have now arrived. Mrs. Mudge is going to show them through, and then perhaps we can finally determined the appropriate punishment for you all."

***

"I can't believe you did something like this," Debbie said as she led Bradley across the school's car park. "What were you thinking?"

"I told you I'm sorry," he replied, before glancing over his shoulder and seeing that Christian and Simon were also being taken home by their parents. The three boys had been dismissed for the day. "We didn't mean for it to all go wrong like this."

"Ghosthunting?" she continued, stopping at the car and turning to him. "Seriously?"

"The ghost of Eve Marsh -"

"There's no such thing as ghosts, Bradley!" she said angrily.

"I saw her!"

"You didn't see anything."

"I saw her, just as clearly as I'm seeing you now!" he replied, struggling to stay patient. He turned and looked toward the field, and he could just about see the old school building in the distance. "She was right in front of me. I even heard her say the name of her old boyfriend. She's in there, and she wants something, and time's running out because soon they're going to knock the place down!"

He looked back over at his mother and saw that she was staring at him incredulously.

"Why don't we go there right now?" he continued. "I'll show you that she's real. You can see her with your own two eyes."

"Is it those comics?" she asked.

"What comics?"

"Those crazy American ones your father's been letting you buy," she continued. "Have they been messing with your head? Or is it something you've been watching on TV? Have you been sneaking downstairs to watch horror films after your grandmother goes to bed?"

"Why won't anyone believe us?" he asked. "We saw the ghost of -"

"There's no such thing as ghosts!" she shouted, stepping toward him, suddenly losing control. "You can't keep going on about this nonsense, Bradley! Ghosts aren't real! When we die, there's just nothing else! Life is life, and when it's over it's over, and nothing you do or say can change that! Death is the end!"

She hesitated, as if she was a little shocked by her own outburst, and then she crouched down in front of him. She looked into his eyes for a moment as she tried to work out exactly what was going through his mind.

"Is this because of me?" she asked finally.

"Why would it be because of you?" he replied, furrowing his brow.

She opened her mouth to reply, but she couldn't quite get the words out.

"It's okay to be scared," she said after moment, reaching out and putting a hand on his shoulder. "If you want to talk about anything, we can talk about it, but what you mustn't do is start going off on these crazy adventures."

"Don't you believe me?"

"Sweetheart -"

"I'm telling you that I saw her," he continued, interrupting her. "She wasn't blurry, she wasn't in the shadows, she was right in front of me. The air was really cold, and I heard her speak, and then she got angry. Christian and Simon saw her too, so it's not like I could have imagined it. Why can't you just believe me? Why won't you come over there with me right now to see for yourself?"

"Because I know the difference between what's actually real, and what I *want* to be real. You need to be able to make that distinction as well, Bradley. As for your punishment, I promised Mr. Ripple that I'm going to find some jobs for you to do around the house. I hope you don't think that you're going to get away with this, because I'm going to make sure that you understand the consequences of your actions. Is that clear?"

"I just want to prove to you that -"

"Not another word," she said firmly. "Get into the car. I can't imagine what your grandmother's going to say when she finds out."

"This totally isn't fair," Bradley muttered under his breath as he climbed into the passenger seat. "We saw the ghost. She's real. Why won't anyone believe us?"

CHAPTER TWENTY

"NO, IT'S FINE," Lou Faraday said as he sat at his desk in the Crowford Gazette's gloomy little office. Posters blocked most of the light from entering through the windows. "Everything's under control."

As he listened to the voice on the other end of the line, he shuffled through some papers.

"That's been taken care of," he continued. "I promise you, all the documents are ash now. The entire situation is in hand, you have nothing to worry about or -"

Hearing the bell ring above the door, he glanced up just in time to see that Dr. Henry Lloyd was entering the building.

"I'll call you back," Lou said, before quickly putting the phone down. "Henry," he continued, feigning being busy as he squinted to get a better look at one of the documents, "to what do I owe the pleasure of another visit so soon?"

"It's Monday," Henry replied, heading over to him. "You told me to come back on Monday, you said you'd have figured out what to do with those papers I gave you."

"I did?" Lou leaned back in his chair for a moment, and then he began to nod slowly. "Right. I remember."

"Well?"

"Well, I'm afraid there's really nothing I *can* do with them," Lou explained. "I realize that's not the answer you wanted, but the truth is, this newspaper isn't set up for campaigning journalism or for poking about in the darkest depths of how the town works. We publish stories about local events, and our readers really don't want to read ghoulish stories about nasty things that happened to respected members of the community."

"So you're just going to bury it all?" Henry replied, horrified by the suggestion.

"No-one's burying anything. I'm simply saying that I can't help you."

Henry stared at him for a moment, clearly taken aback.

"I should have known," he said finally. "Fine, Lou, have it your way, but I *will* be taking this further. I don't know who I'll go to, but there has to be someone out there who'll listen to me.

Give me the documents back and I'll figure it out on my own."

"Oh, did you want them back?" Lou replied. "I'm sorry, Henry, I didn't realize that. I was having a clear-out the other day and I'm afraid those documents got mixed up in all of that. They all ended up being incinerated."

"You destroyed them?"

"You had other copies, right?"

"I told you I didn't!" Henry snapped angrily. "The only other copies are with the police, and I can't exactly waltz in there and get more without arousing suspicion. I explicitly told you all of this the other day, Lou!"

"You did?" Lou furrowed his brow for a moment. "I must have missed that part."

"Did you even look at them properly?"

"I gave them all the attention they deserved," Lou said, struggling to contain a smile. "I must admit, it wasn't nice seeing those awful photos of Alan Walton's body. I've seen plenty of nasty pictures over the years, but it's different when it's someone you know. If you want my advice, Henry, you'll drop this rubbish and get on with something else. Relax. Get a drink. Have a cigarette."

"And pretend that everything was completely normal with Alan's death?"

"Works for me," Lou said with a shrug.

"Crowford's a nice sleepy little town, and I think we all have a duty to make sure that it stays that way. You've lived here long enough to know not to stir the pot, Henry, haven't you?"

"Unbelievable," Henry replied, taking a step back. "There's a nasty little gang in Crowford, isn't there? Who else is part of the little cabal that makes sure the truth gets buried?"

"I don't know what you're talking about," Lou said. "You're sounding a little bit like one of those conspiracy theorists, though. Take a chill pill, Henry, and focus on the good things in life. Trust me, you'll never look back!"

"You didn't see the inside of that school building," Henry told him. "You didn't see the markings on the walls. The truth is there, and the truth is going to find its way out one way or another. You and your friends, whoever they are, can only stand in the way for so long."

***

"I want to see that homework completed in one hour," Debbie called up the stairs as Bradley headed to his room. "Just because you're getting the afternoon off school, that doesn't mean you're going to sit around doing nothing."

She waited, but Bradley slammed his bedroom door shut, and Debbie sighed as she headed through to the kitchen. As soon as she reached the doorway, however, she was startled by the sight of her mother sitting at the table.

"I didn't realize you were here," Debbie said, before wandering over to the counter.

She began to make a cup of tea. As soon as she turned to ask her mother if she wanted one, however, she saw that there were tears running down Josephine's face.

"Mum?" she said cautiously, before heading over to her. "What's the matter?"

Josephine looked up at her, and for a moment she seemed lost for words.

"Sit down, darling," she said finally. "Debbie, please... I think I need to tell you something, and I want to do it now because otherwise I might back down and then you'll never know the truth."

"What are you talking about? Mum, I've had a hell of a day, I just had to go to the school and -"

"It's about your father."

Debbie hesitated, before taking a seat opposite her.

"What about him?" she asked cautiously. She waited, and now she was starting to feel a sense of dread slowly creeping through her chest. "Dad's been dead for a long time now," she continued. "It'll be fourteen years soon. I miss him every day."

Again she waited, but Josephine seemed

almost to have frozen as fresh tears filled her eyes.

"Your father was the best man I ever met," Josephine said finally. "Kind. Honest. Understanding. When Bernard died, a part of me died with him. And I will never, ever forget the tenderness he showed me after I..."

Her voice trailed off.

"After you *what*, Mum?"

"It was 1953," Josephine continued. "Oh, that feels like a world away now. Your father and I had been married for seven years. We'd been trying for a baby, but we hadn't had a great deal of luck. Still, we were young and we knew we had plenty of time. Our life together was so happy, although my mother – your grandmother – had a nasty fall that summer and I had to spend a lot of time over there, helping her out."

"Was that after Granddad died?"

Josephine nodded.

"Okay." Debbie hesitated. "Where's this story going, Mum?"

"I was walking home from Grandma's house late one night," Josephine said, "and I took a shortcut through the park. I don't know why I was so foolish, but I just wanted to get home. There were no lights in the park back then, but it was only supposed to take me a few minutes to go that way and I'd never felt unsafe in Crowford, not in all my years." She paused. "And then... someone grabbed me."

"What do you mean?" Debbie asked. "Grabbed you *how*?"

"Don't make me spell it out, dear," she replied. "It was so dark, I didn't even see his face, all I could tell was that he was older than me. When I got home, I tried to pretend that nothing had happened, but of course Bernard saw through all of that. I had cuts and bruises, and I was shaking."

"You never told me this before."

"We swore we wouldn't," Josephine replied, "but with everything that's been going on, and after talking to Alan Walton the other day, just before he died, I suddenly feel as if I can't keep it in." She made the sign of the cross against her chest. "Oh Bernard," she whispered, "please forgive me."

"Mum, I'm so sorry that this happened to you, but -"

"It was Michael Archer," she said suddenly.

"The man who attacked you?"

Josephine nodded.

"I didn't see his face," she continued, "but it didn't take much to work it out. He was still around in those days, and everyone knew that he was up to no good, although he tended to cause most of his trouble outside Crowford. That's one of the reasons why I felt so safe. No-one thought he'd ever do anything here in our little town, not again."

"Michael Archer attacked you?"

Josephine nodded again.

"Mum, that's so awful," Debbie said, reaching across the table and squeezing her hand tight. "I can see why the talk of Eve Marsh has reopened some old wounds for you, but -"

"Let me finish," Josephine replied through gritted teeth, "or I might never say it."

"Say what?"

"Bernard and I decided to put it behind us," she continued. "We reported the matter to the police, but we knew they wouldn't ever act. Besides, we had no proof that it was him. You must also remember that times were different back then. There was more shame. We were expected to just get on with things. So we did, your father and I, until..."

Her voice trailed off.

"Until what, Mum?" Debbie asked.

"Until nine months later," Josephine replied, her voice trembling with fear, "when *you* were born."

CHAPTER TWENTY-ONE

HEARING RAISED VOICES DOWN in the kitchen, Bradley stopped at the top of the stairs and listened for a moment. He could tell that something was wrong, and he didn't like the idea that his mother and grandmother might be upset. After a few seconds he began to make his way down to the hallway, but at that moment Debbie stormed through and grabbed her coat from the rack.

"What's wrong?" Bradley asked.

"Nothing," Debbie said, wiping away tears.

"Mum..."

"I'm just going out for an hour or two," Debbie added, opening the door and stepping outside. "Do your homework and I'll check it when I get home."

"But -"

"And I don't want any arguments," she said. "You've caused more than enough trouble already today, young man, and I really need you to just cooperate."

With that, Debbie slammed the door shut, leaving Bradley standing alone. He listened to the sound of his mother's footsteps hurrying away, and then he turned and made his way through to the door that led into the kitchen. Stopping, he saw that Josephine was sitting with her head in her hands.

"Nana?" he said cautiously. "Are you and Mum okay?"

Josephine looked at him.

"Of course, darling," she said unconvincingly. "Your mother's just a little upset about something, that's all."

"Is she angry at you?"

"She's just reacting to some news, that's all. There's something I should have told her a long time ago, and I think she needs a little while to come to terms with it. But it's nothing for you to worry about. I'll make you some tea soon. Would you like a burger?"

"What did you tell Mum?"

"Nothing, dear," Josephine said, before holding a hand out toward him. "Nothing for you to worry yourself about. Come here."

Bradley made his way over to her, and to his surprise he found himself pulled into a tight hug.

"Adults do and say the wrong thing sometimes," Josephine said. "We twist ourselves into knots, and untwisting those knots can be very difficult. We convince ourselves that the truth is what's most important, but right now I'm not sure whether that's really true. I think perhaps I should have let it all be."

"I heard you talking about Michael Archer," Bradley replied. "Why were you arguing about *him*?"

"It's more complicated than that."

"But he's dead, isn't he?"

"Yes, dear. He's gone."

"So why would you argue about him? What's the point?" He paused. "I know he killed Eve Marsh. He's the man she called Adam, isn't he?"

"Michael Archer was a wicked man," Josephine replied, letting go of him and sitting back. "That's all you need to know. He was dreadful, and all of Crowford should be glad that he's dead. I know that might sound like an awful thing to say, but I'm afraid it's true." She wiped some more tears away as she got to her feet and headed to the fridge. "How about scrambled eggs? Would you like that?"

Without waiting for an answer, she started taking items from the fridge. Bradley headed through to the front room and lifted the net curtains so that he could see outside, but there was no sign of his mother. He wanted to run after her, but he had no idea which way she'd gone. Sitting on the edge of the sofa, he looked at the coffee table and saw a pile of documents along with a portable tape recorder and a few other items from Debbie's days as a reporter.

Reaching over, he opened one of the folders and found some newspaper cuttings. He started looking through them, and then he froze as he saw one that mentioned the death of Michael Archer.

"Mr. Archer is believed to have been living in an abandoned farmhouse near Hovington," he whispered as he read the cutting, "about ten miles outside Crowford. Locals claims that he lived as a recluse, venturing out only to purchase essential supplies from nearby shops."

He paused for a moment.

"Hovington," he murmured, as he remembered that he and his mother had driven past that little village on their way to Crossley Morton a few days earlier. He even remembered spotting what had looked like an abandoned building in the distance, near the crossroads by the petrol station. Had Michael Archer, the awful man who'd killed Eve Marsh, been living there all along, until his death?

"Come and set the table!" Josephine called through to him. "Come now, Bradley!"

***

"Do people always haunt the place where they died?" Bradley asked a little while later, as he finished the last of his scrambled eggs.

"I'm sorry?" Josephine replied.

"If someone dies," he continued, "and they're a mean person, or for some reason they're going to haunt somewhere, is it always the place where they died?"

"I really wouldn't know, dear," she said, before glancing through to the front room. She'd been waiting for Debbie to return, so that she could make things right, but she was starting to think that her daughter was going to be out for a while.

"It makes sense, though, doesn't it?" Bradley said. "I don't suppose ghosts can choose where to haunt, or why would Eve Marsh -"

"I think we should talk about something else," Josephine replied, interrupting him. "No-one wants to talk about ghosts, do they? Especially not now."

"Michael Archer was a bad man, wasn't he?"

"Eat your tea."

"But he -"

"Just eat your tea!" Josephine snapped angrily, before taking a deep breath and focusing. "I'm sorry, that was uncalled for, but I don't want to talk about that man. Not now, not ever again. He's caused too much pain."

"Sorry," Bradley murmured as he looked back down at his eggs.

The rest of the meal was silent, since Bradley knew better than to risk saying anything that might upset his grandmother. He still didn't know exactly what had caused the argument between Josephine and his mother, but he could feel the tension in the air and he knew that he wouldn't be able to help. He supposed that he should simply go up to his room and get on with his homework, but in the back of his mind he couldn't help but still feel annoyed that his mother hadn't believed him when he'd told her about the ghost of Eve Marsh. He, Christian and Simon had been so close to gaining proof of the ghost's existence, but they'd fallen short.

"Nana," he said finally, "in a minute, can I call Christian? It's about my homework."

"Okay, but be quick," she replied. "That phone bill has been growing out of hand."

"Thank you," he said, trying his best to be polite so that he wouldn't draw any attention to himself. "I'll wash the dishes first, though."

Twenty minutes later, sitting on the stairs, he waited while Christian's mother went to fetch her son. His mind was racing and he was more and more certain that it was too soon to give up, that he and the others had to try again to get the proof that they so desperately needed. By the time Christian finally picked up the phone, Bradley was starting to fidget with nerves.

"I'm not allowed out to play for a month," Christian complained. "Don't you think that's totally unfair? I could understand a week, but a month is like the most extreme form of punishment you can get. I don't even think it's legal."

"We have to go back," Bradley said firmly. "To the school, I mean."

"I can't. I told you, I'm grounded. So's Simon."

"Then I'm going back by myself," Bradley told him. "I'm going to prove to everyone that Eve Marsh's ghost is there."

"That's crazy," Christian replied. "She's angry, Bradley. If you go back, she'll hurt you, just like she hurt other people."

"Then what can I do?"

"If you could figure out *why* she's angry," Christian continued, "then you'd have something to offer her. That way, you could help her, and at the same time it'd be much easier for you to get a good photo of her."

"How do I do that?" Bradley replied, unable to shake a sense of frustration. "It's not like she's given us any clues. She just seems mad about the fact that she was murdered. You saw the way she'd scratched the name Adam into all the walls in there, she's totally focused on her boyfriend, but he's the one who killed her. It's almost as if..."

His voice trailed off, and he realized after a moment that he had one other option.

"As if *what*?" Christian asked.

"I've got it," Bradley replied, although he could feel a sense of real fear tightening in his chest. "I can't believe it took me this long to figure it out. I know *exactly* what I have to do."

CHAPTER TWENTY-TWO

"I'M SO SORRY FOR just turning up unannounced like this," Debbie said as she stepped into the hallway of Julie's house. "I really need to talk to someone. Mum just dropped a massive bombshell on me and -"

Stopping suddenly, she saw Dr. Henry Lloyd sitting on the sofa.

"Oh," Debbie continued, turning to Julie, "you have company. I'm sorry, I can go and find someone else to talk to."

"No, it's fine," Julie replied, already shutting the door. "In fact, I was thinking of calling you this evening anyway. Henry came to me because we met a few times back when I worked for the paper. He's told me some pretty troubling things this afternoon and we're trying to figure out where to go from here." She paused. "What's wrong, Debbie? You look like you've seen a ghost."

"I'll tell you later."

"You heard about Alan Walton, right?" Julie said, leading her over to the other sofa. "He was found dead at the school."

"I know," Debbie replied, as she saw several documents laid out on the coffee table. "It's all people have been whispering and muttering about in town all day, I've overheard enough crazy theories to make your head spin. Is there any news about what actually happened?"

"I've submitted my report," Henry told her, "but I'm afraid that's not going to do very much to bring the truth to light. I also took some items to Lou Faraday at the Crowford Gazette, and he proceeded to destroy them so that none of the information could get out. I always had my suspicions about that man, and unfortunately those suspicions have now been confirmed."

"I don't understand," Debbie said. "What exactly's going on?"

"I lied to Lou about the documents," Henry explained, as he looked back down at the documents. "Partly, at least. I told him that I didn't have time to copy any more of them, but the truth is that I managed to photocopy the ones that I thought were particularly important. Lou might think that he's successfully hidden what happened, but I have photos that prove otherwise."

"Are those from the autopsy?" Debbie asked, stepping around the table so that she could get a better look. She set her bag down and then sat on the edge of the sofa, and when she picked up the nearest photo she was shocked by the sight of Alan Walton's dead face with the name Adam scratched all over his features. "Who did that to him?"

"I would dearly like to know," Henry replied.

"That's not the strangest thing, though," Julie said. "Henry, show her *the* photo."

Henry hesitated, before sliding one particular picture out from the bottom of the pile.

"It's standard practice," he said, "to remove the brain during an autopsy. For one thing, it has to be weighed."

"You're not about to tell me that the name Adam was scratched into his brain, are you?" Debbie asked.

"Not his brain." He held the photo up for her to see, although for a moment she couldn't quite make the image out. "Somehow, that name had been scratched on the inside of the man's skull, over and over."

Taking the photo, Debbie finally realized that it showed the inside of Alan's skull. The brain had been taken out, but she could see lots of scratches that had been left in the bone, many of which spelled out the name Adam.

"I cut that man's head open myself," Henry continued, "and I can assure you that nobody else had access to do something like this. There is absolutely no way that those marks could possibly have been put there before Alan Walton arrived on my table, but there they are, for all to see. Now, tell me how anyone could do something like that to the man."

"There has to be an explanation," Debbie pointed out. "There just *has* to be, otherwise..."

"I think you see what's troubling us now," Julie told her. "I don't think Lou's the only one in Crowford who wants all of this to get swept under the rug. Lou's a lazy man, he's doing this because he's following orders. And my guess is that he's been following those orders for a very long time. He's probably not the only one, either. Debbie, I think we're looking at proof that something very bad has been going on in Crowford for years. Maybe even since before we were born."

***

"Michael Archer's your *father*?" Julie said incredulously as she and Debbie sat smoking on the back step. "Are you sure?"

"Unless Mum suddenly developed a really sick sense of humor," Debbie replied, "then yeah, apparently Dad – I mean, Bernard – wasn't my biological father. My biological father was that murderous bastard Archer. And apparently we can add rape to his list of crimes. I mean, she didn't see his face, but she's certain."

"Why did she decide to tell you this now?"

"I think she's just been holding it in for decades," Debbie explained, "and a few things recently have set her off." She paused, staring out across the dark garden. "I bit her head off," she continued. "Instead of consoling her and listening to her, I just stormed out of there. Does that make me a bitch?"

"Not at all."

"It's just so hard to believe that Dad isn't my dad at all."

"Hey, he's the one who raised you," Julie pointed out. "Nothing can ever change that."

"I'm just starting to see how all of this is linked," Debbie replied. "Crowford's supposed to be this nice quiet little town, but there's actually some kind of web of nastiness and misery that's hanging just out of sight."

"Are you sure you're not exaggerating a little?"

"I don't think I am," Debbie said. "Michael Archer must have been one of the sickest, most depraved individuals who ever lived, and forces in this town conspired to protect him."

"He was driven out. He never got to come back."

"That's not justice," Debbie replied, before taking another drag on her cigarette. "That's convenience. The great and the good of Crowford, whoever they might be, decided that they didn't want their precious little town's name to be tainted. Obviously they turned a blind eye to what Michael Archer was doing for as long as they were able, and then when he became too much for them to handle, they shipped him off. And what we know about is probably only the tip of the iceberg. I can't even begin to imagine what else he might have done."

"Such as?"

"Do you really think he murdered Eve Marsh and nobody else?" she asked. "Do you really think my mother was the only woman he attacked?"

"But -"

"And the police did nothing!" Debbie added. "Mum and Dad didn't even press it that hard. Mum said she felt so ashamed, she begged Dad to keep it all quiet and they pretended that he was my father. As for Dad, he would have done whatever he thought was best for our family. I'm sure he wanted to make Michael Archer pay, but he probably realized that there was nothing he could do. Dad was a shoe salesman. What could a shoe salesman possibly do to take down a member of the Archer family?"

"Meanwhile, Lou didn't only help to keep the truth out of the paper," Julie pointed out. "He's okay with actively suppressing evidence. Henry came to me tonight because he didn't know where else to turn. The problem is, *I* don't know where to turn either. If the Crowford Gazette won't take the story, I don't see that there are any other outlets. The nationals aren't going to be interested, not unless we can come up with significantly more proof. It's beyond frustrating, but I just can't figure out what to do next."

"Do you ever feel like there's way more to Crowford than you see on the surface?" Debbie asked. "It's as if there's this dark heart that beats in the shadows, and nobody notices it, or they pretend not to. If you think about it, Crowford has had way more than its fair share of tragedy. We've had several real disasters in this town. Meanwhile, there's this corruption that's also going on behind the scenes, first with the Archers and then with the Graces, and what else has been swept away out of sight? I don't know if I'm imagining things, Julie, but I'm starting to really worry about this town. I'm starting to worry about Bradley growing up here."

"Crowford isn't *that* bad," Julie replied.

"Then explain this," Debbie said, holding up the photo of the inside of Alan Walton's skull. "Explain how something so awful could happen, because I'm at a loss. And the worst part is that whatever we're going up against is so big, and so entrenched, that..." Her voice trailed off for a moment. "I just don't see," she added finally, "that we have any hope of changing anything at all."

CHAPTER TWENTY-THREE

"I'M COMPLETELY CONFIDENT," Lou Faraday said, sitting alone in his office. "Henry Lloyd isn't going to be a problem, not anymore."

He listened for a moment to the voice on the other end of the phone.

"I understand," he continued, "but there's really no need to worry. And the school building is getting knocked down really soon. You managed to get that moved forward, and I don't see any reason for delays. Over the next couple of days, the engineers are going to go in there for their final checks and -"

The voice interrupted him, and Lou couldn't help but roll his eyes as he listened.

"Such as?" he asked.

He listened again.

"I really don't see how," he continued. "All that's written on those walls is the name Adam, over and over. Nothing else, nothing incriminating. My advice would be -"

The voice interrupted him yet again, and Lou sighed as he leaned back in his chair and listened to what turned out to be a lengthy diatribe.

"Fine," he muttered, "then send someone."

He listened, and then he sat forward.

"Why me?" he asked, shocked by the suggestion.

The voice ranted for a few seconds.

"Well, I *might* have better things to do," he said indignantly. "I'm sure you have plenty of people you can ask to go and take a look. I'm busy and it's late and I'd really rather just get on with getting the next issue ready. The news never -"

Interrupted again, he listened as the voice went on and on, and he already knew deep down that he was in no position to put up much of a fight.

"Fine," he said, as he looked down at his papers. "Of course you're right, I *do* appreciate the fact that you've stood behind me and given me the opportunity to edit this marvelous newspaper. And I don't mind doing a few little side jobs for you. I have to finish a couple of things here, and then I'll see what I can do. I honestly don't think that you need to worry, though. This little mess is over. And once that old school is torn down, the whole thing will be put to bed once and for all."

***

"Hey, Mum."

Looking up from her magazine, Josephine saw Debbie standing in the doorway.

"You're home," Josephine said, her voice tight with emotion. "Bradley's gone to bed, so I'll head off. I should sleep at my house tonight."

She got to her feet, but Debbie immediately rushed over and hugged her tight.

"I'm so sorry, Mum," she sobbed. "I can't believe I reacted the way I did. I can't believe I acted like it was your fault for not telling me sooner." She pulled her even tighter. "I can't believe you've been carrying this secret around for all these years. I can't believe Dad kept it hidden."

She stepped back and saw tears in her mother's eyes.

"Your father and I are from a different generation," Josephine pointed out. "We're not quite as open with our emotions as you youngsters of the 1980's. We faced a challenge, and we dealt with it." She paused. "And I don't want you to ever think that your father was any less of a father to you, just because biologically he... Well, you know what I mean."

"He was the best father anyone could ever

have wished for," Debbie replied, "and I miss him every single day."

"So do I, darling." Josephine sniffed back some more tears. "And now, if you don't mind, I must go up to the bathroom and tidy myself up. Would you mind putting the kettle on for me? When I get back down, I'll be happy to answer any questions you might have."

Debbie watched as her mother headed through to the hallway. She wanted to go after her, to tell her again and again that she was sorry for how she'd reacted, but she supposed there'd be time for that later. As she made her way over to the kettle, however, she spotted a letter resting on the sideboard. Picking the letter up, she saw her own name on the front, and a mark on the envelope that indicated it was from Andelam Hospital. She froze for a moment, before quickly opening the letter and taking a look.

As soon as she saw that it was from Doctor Sanders, begging her to return to the ward, she scrunched the letter up and threw it straight into the bin.

"I don't know how to make this any clearer to you, Deborah," she remembered Doctor Sanders telling her a few days earlier. "You're putting yourself in terrible danger. Now, I can't stop you, but I have to warn you of the potential consequences, not only for you but for your family."

"I know the consequences," she'd told him.

"Do you? Do you realize that you could become extremely ill at any moment? Do you realize that a member of your family could find you and it might already be too late?"

"I'm only going for a week," she'd insisted. "Maybe two. Then I'll come back and you can fill me up with all the chemo in the world again. I just need to go home, at least for a little while. It might be my last chance."

"If we can get you back into remission -"

"That's never going to happen, is it?" she'd asked him, and she remembered that the look in his eyes had told her that she was right. "I'm not going to beat this thing," she'd added. "You can't say it to my face, but we all know I'm getting worse and worse. I'll fight this thing until my last breath, but I know impossible odds when I see them. And I refuse to die without at least having one normal trip home first."

Upstairs, her mother flushed the toilet.

Realizing that she'd allowed herself to become distracted, Debbie set the kettle on to boil and then laid out two cups. As her mother returned, however, she remembered how harsh she'd been with Bradley, and she realized that she owed her son an apology.

"That's better," Josephine said. "Now, I think I have some cake in the fridge, would you like a slice?"

"Sure," Debbie replied, stepping past her, "but I want to go up and check on Bradley first."

"I think you'll find that he's asleep."

"I know," she said, stopping in the doorway and turning back to her mother, "but I was pretty tough on him earlier. After the stunt he and his friends pulled at school today, he kind of deserved it, but I might have gone slightly too far."

"He's a good boy, you know," Josephine replied.

"I know. I'm so proud of him."

"And he's resilient, too," Josephine continued. "He gets that from you."

Smiling, Debbie turned and headed upstairs. Her legs felt a little weak, and she had to pause halfway up the stairs in order to get her strength. By the time she reached Bradley's room and pushed the door open, she needed to stop again, and she couldn't help but note that she was becoming more frail by the day. She was almost at the end of her first week back at home, which meant she should be thinking about going back to the hospital. At the same time, that thought filled her with dread, since she knew that she'd probably never make it out again.

One more week, she told herself, *and then it's time.*

Spotting a shape under the duvet on

Bradley's bed, she watched for a moment as her son slept. She knew she should leave him alone, that he had to get up early in the morning for school, but she was starting to think that she might let him have a day off. She'd been so strict, and now she felt that she could at least steal him away for one little trip somewhere. They wouldn't have to go far, just to the pier and the beach, but she wanted one last day with her son, one carefree chance to potter around the streets of Crowford and just pretend to be normal.

Finally, figuring that she should let him know her decision, she crept over to the bed and leaned down to nudge him awake.

"Bradley," she whispered, "I -"

Suddenly realizing that something was wrong, she pulled the duvet down a little and saw to her horror that Bradley was missing. Several pillows had been arranged under the duvet to form the rough approximation of a human shape, but as she looked around the room she saw no sign of Bradley at all.

Filled with panic, she hurried out onto the landing and then down the stairs, and it was at that moment that she noticed her son's coat and shoes were also missing.

"Mum!" she called out. "Bradley's gone!"

CHAPTER TWENTY-FOUR

THE BUS DOORS HISSED open and Bradley stepped down onto the pavement. He looked out at the darkness all around, and then he turned to look back up at the driver.

"And you live here?" the man asked skeptically.

Bradley nodded.

"I don't see many houses around," the man pointed out.

"I live right over there," Bradley told him, nodding in the vague direction of the petrol station. "My parents are expecting me."

"Alright, then. See that you hurry home."

"I will. Thank you."

With that, Bradley made his way to the crossing. He could tell that the driver was still watching him, and as he headed to the other side of the road he began to wonder just when the man would drive away. A moment later, he heard the bus doors hiss shut, and then as he started walking toward the petrol station he heard the bus setting off again. He turned, just as the bus roared past, and then he stopped and watched as the vehicle disappeared into the night.

Shivering slightly in the cold, Bradley pulled his coat tighter before turning and heading back across the road. He passed the bus stop, and then he stopped at the edge of the field. He couldn't see anything in the distance, of course, but he knew exactly where he was going so he clambered over the low stone wall and set off across the mud.

***

Half an hour later, after trudging through thick mud that was making his ankles ache, Bradley aimed the flashlight ahead and finally saw the side of the little farmhouse.

He stopped, turning the flashlight slightly, and he felt a shudder pass through his bones as he looked at the pitch-black single-storey building and realized that he'd found what he'd been looking for. After reading the notes in his mother's pile of clippings, he'd located the house where Michael Archer had spent his final years.

It was also the house where, a few months earlier, Michael Archer had died alone and almost forgotten.

Bradley swallowed hard. He knew that he was taking a huge risk, but he was determined to get some proof of the existence of ghosts. He also knew that if he was ever going to go back to the school and face Eve Marsh again, he needed to be able to offer her something. He'd thought long and hard about what a ghost might want, and finally – while he'd been talking to Christian – he'd realized that he could try to offer Eve some kind of satisfaction regarding her death. If Michael Archer had killed her, then it was Michael Archer whose confession might bring an end to all the suffering.

Reaching into his pocket, he double-checked that he had the tape recorder, and then he started making his way along the farmhouse's side, searching for the entrance.

Once he'd found the door, he stopped and listened for a moment. He'd never heard so much silence before, and he worried that even the slightest noise might draw attention. At the same time, he reminded himself that he'd made the journey specifically because he *wanted* to talk to the ghost of Michael Archer, and he also reminded himself that he had a plan to make sure that he'd stay safe.

Reaching out, he tried the handle, and to his

surprise he found that the door was unlocked. He pushed, and the door creaked open, revealing the darkness of the cottage's interior. Raising the flashlight, he immediately saw that the cottage was actually in better condition that he'd expected, with basic furniture as well as some pictures hanging on the walls.

He edged forward, but he was careful to make sure that he didn't cross the threshold and actually enter the cottage. After all, he'd figured that so long as he stayed outside, no ghost could get to him.

Assuming, of course, that Michael Archer's ghost was still around, of course.

Taking the tape recorder from his pocket, Bradley pressed the button to start recording. His hands were trembling slightly as he heard the hiss of the machine whirring to life, and then he held the recorder as close to the open doorway as he dared.

He opened his mouth to speak, and then he hesitated.

The flashlight's beam was dancing across the far wall, picking out a crack that ran from the floor to the ceiling.

"Hello?" Bradley said finally, unable to keep the fear from his voice. "Is anyone there? I'm looking for... I mean... I'm here to speak to Michael Archer. To the ghost of Michael Archer. If you're here, please say something."

He waited, but all he heard was the continued hum of the recorder.

"I want to speak to Michael Archer," he continued. "My name's Bradley Firth and I've come out here tonight from Crowford. I want to talk to you about..."

His voice trailed off. He was worried about angering the ghost, but he knew he had to be brave. He looked down again at his feet and saw that he was still a good few inches from the threshold of the cottage.

"I want to talk to you about Eve Marsh," he said finally, as he once again looked into the cottage. "She died at the school a long time ago, and she's still there. I mean, she's dead, but I saw her today. She's trapped there and the school's going to be knocked down soon, so time's running out to help her."

He listened.

Nothing.

"You *want* to help her, don't you?" he asked. "I know you're the one who murdered her, but don't you want to set that right? This is a chance for you to redeem yourself."

He listened.

Again, he heard no response.

He took a deep breath, and then he decided to take a slight risk. He strengthened his grip on the flashlight, and then he very slowly began to peer around the edge of the door. He was leaning across the threshold now, into the cottage, but he told himself that he'd be fine so long as his feet didn't actually go through. Tilting the flashlight around, he aimed it toward the other end of the room and saw what appeared to be a sofa, along with books on shelves. Again, he was surprised to find that Michael Archer had been living in a fairly decent place.

"Hello?" he called out, looking at one of the armchairs, half expecting to see a ghostly figure materialize. "My name's Bradley and I'm here to see Michael Archer, I want -"

Before he could finish, he heard a faint bumping sound. Letting out a gasp, he pulled back and made sure his entire body was outside the cottage again, and then he listened out for any further hint of movement.

"Come on," he whispered, "I know you're here somewhere. You have to be. If *anyone* haunted the place where they died, it'd be someone like Michael Archer."

As those words left his lips, however, he was starting to think that he might have made a miscalculation. What if Michael Archer wasn't haunting the cottage at all? What if his spirit had simply departed after his death, or what if the rules were different and he was haunting somewhere else? Bradley was starting to realize how many assumptions he'd made and how little he really understood, but at the same time he'd spent an hour on the bus and he wasn't ready to go home empty-handed.

Not yet.

Still, he knew that he needed to try a different approach.

"I saw Eve Marsh today," he said, raising his voice a little in order to make sure that he could be heard throughout the cottage. "She's trapped in that school, and she's written your name on all the walls. Well, she's written the name Adam, which is the name she used for you. I think she's really upset, and I think you should do the right thing and let me record a message from you. If you could tell her that you're sorry, if she could hear those words coming from your mouth, she might finally be set free."

He waited.

After a couple of seconds, he heard a faint rustling sound, but he couldn't quite work out where it was coming from. He aimed the flashlight all around, but the rustling sound had already stopped. Had it been over by the sofa, or more toward the door that led into another part of the cottage? Once again, Bradley began to lean a little forward, across the threshold, but after a moment he stopped himself. He craned his neck to get a better view through into the kitchen, and then – realizing that he was in danger of falling inside – he stepped back.

"My name is Bradley Firth," he continued, even though he was starting to think that no-one was listening, "and I'm here to talk to the ghost of Michael Archer, about the ghost of Eve Marsh. It's really important, so if you're here, I'm begging you to -"

Suddenly he heard a twig snap nearby. He spun around, and in that moment he saw a tall, dark figure looming over him, silhouetted against the night sky. Before he could react, he felt a hand press hard against his chest, shoving him against the wall. The flashlight fell from his hand, and he caught a quick glimpse of an old, lined, angry face staring at him.

"Who are you?" the old man sneered. "What are you doing here, and what's all this nonsense about ghosts?"

CHAPTER TWENTY-FIVE

"I... I... I..."

For a moment, Bradley could only stare in horror at the old man. After a couple of seconds, however, he felt the hand pull away from his chest. Stumbling to the side, Bradley immediately tripped on the doorstep and fell back, toppling into the cottage and landing hard on the stone floor.

"I asked you a question, boy," the old man said, filling the doorway, blocking any chance of escape. "What are you doing coming to my home so late at night?"

Too scared to speak, Bradley scrambled to his feet and turned, racing through into the next room. He bumped against the counter-top, and then he spotted a door at the far end of the kitchen.

Racing over, he pulled it open, only to find that the old man was waiting right outside.

"Boy, you won't -"

Screaming, Bradley turned to run again. This time, however, his right foot caught on the leg of a table and he fell, slamming hard against the ground and slithering headfirst into a kitchen cabinet. The impact was hard enough to send a jolt through his body, and he let out a faint murmur as he tried to sit up. For a moment, feeling dizzy, he could only turn and watch as the old man stepped over to join him.

"You dropped this," the man said, reaching down and handing him the flashlight. "Now, how about you stop running around like a headless chicken, huh? Do you want to start by telling me what the bloody hell's going on here?"

***

Sitting at the kitchen table, with a pack of ice pressed against his forehead, Bradley kept his eyes fixed on the old man. The cottage's lights were on now, and the man – who looked to be in his late seventies at least, perhaps even his eighties – had let out a pained groan as he'd taken a seat opposite.

"What did you say your name was, again?"

the man asked. "Bradley?"

"Who are you?" Bradley replied.

"Well, my name is Michael."

"Michael Archer?"

The man hesitated, and then he nodded.

"And you're..." For a moment, Bradley couldn't quite bring himself to get the next words out. "You're a ghost. Aren't you?"

"Do I look like a ghost?"

"You..."

Bradley's voice trailed off for a few seconds.

"You're lucky I happened to be awake," Michael replied. "I don't sleep well these days. I was on my bed when I heard you calling out and, well, to be honest I tend to be very skeptical about visitors. I don't want any."

The old man hesitated, before slowly sliding his right hand across the table.

"Do I feel like a ghost?"

Bradley looked down at his hand.

"Well," Michael continued, "*do* I?"

Bradley began to reach out, but he couldn't quite bring himself to actually touch the man.

"Don't worry," Michael said, pulling his hand back, "you're not crazy. The truth is, everyone thinks I'm dead, which is how I want things to be. Earlier in the year, I set about making sure that word spread of my untimely demise. It wasn't too hard to make people believe that I'd died, and it's not like anyone was going to want to come to my funeral. I faked the whole thing."

"So you're not a ghost?" Bradley asked, as he felt a sense of dread rising through his chest.

"If you'd lived the kind of life I've lived," Michael replied, "you might be tempted to pull the same stunt. For decades, my name has been mud all around this county. People have talked and gossiped about me, they blamed me for the most awful things. I suppose I became curious in the end, I wanted to know if anything would change once they thought I was dead and buried. I hoped that the hatred might fade a little, and that the truth might come out. That's not what happened, though. Aside from a brief mention in that pathetic rag of a newspaper, my supposed death didn't draw much attention at all. I suppose you could say that the experiment failed and -"

Suddenly he broke into a cough, and it took him several tries to clear his throat. He grabbed a tissue and wiped his hands, but the cough seemed to be coming from deep down in his chest.

"It'll become true soon enough, though," he added, struggling to speak. "I'm eighty-two years old and I haven't exactly looked after myself. I don't have long left in this world."

Bradley stared at him, still trying to figure out exactly what was happening.

"So you came all this way out here to find me, did you?" Michael asked. "No offense, but you don't really look old enough to be doing something like that on your own. You're from Crowford, I believe you said. Do your parents know what you're up to?"

"Not exactly."

"Not exactly." A faint smile crossed Michael's lips. "My old car's not in any fit state, I'm afraid, and I don't have a phone. How did you get here?"

"Bus," Bradley stammered. "I... took the bus."

"You won't find one going back," Michael told him, "not this late. The next one'll be around six in the morning. You didn't think about that, did you?"

Again, Bradley swallowed hard.

"You mentioned a name," Michael continued. "When you were calling out earlier, you mentioned a name that I haven't heard in a very long time. You said something about Eve Marsh."

"She's the woman you killed!"

"Careful with accusations like that,"

Michael said. "You don't want to believe everything you read in the Crowford Gazette."

"Everyone knows you did it."

"And everyone's wrong!" Michael snapped, momentarily showing a burst of anger before starting to cough again. He took a moment to regather his composure. "You've no idea, young man, of the amount of pure horseshit that's been talked about me over the years. Do you know who I am? Who I *really* am, I mean. Do you know about my family, about how the Archers once owned half of Crowford?"

"I know some of it."

"It's a long way down from where my father was, to where I am today." Michael paused, with sadness in his eyes. "I'm no victim. I don't want anyone to feel sorry for me. What happened to my family, and to me, was entirely my fault, and I won't try to shift the blame. I was a disgrace. I was born into a life of luxury and wealth, and I pissed it all away. Pardon my language there. But my point is, despite everything I just told you, my only crime was to be a weak and pathetic man. Everything else they said about me – the attacks, the violence, the horrible things that were done to people in Crowford – was a lie. I never hurt another soul. Well, not physically, at least."

"You killed Eve Marsh."

"No," Michael said, shaking his head, "I did not."

"Everyone knows!"

"Because everyone's been fed a pack of lies," Michael sneered, "that's been spread about for more than half a century! That bastard Eric Grace destroyed my family, and he used me to do it, and I was too drunk and stupid and naive to stop him! Every bad thing that happened in Crowford was blamed on me, and I couldn't do a damn thing about that fact. Even my own father believed the lies, and he was destroyed by all that shame. Eventually I was run out of town, and do you know what? I didn't even fight it. I let the bastards win."

"Everyone knows that you killed her," Bradley replied. "It's just a fact. I mean, everyone in Crowford talks about what you did. Not just that, but all the other things too."

"I'm sure it seems that way, to a child," Michael replied. "You have that excuse. Everyone else in Crowford just believed what they wanted to believe. Instead of accepting that various people had done bad things, they lumped all the sins of the town onto me. I suppose I can understand the lure of that, in a way. It was easy. It allowed them to pretend that the problem could be easily solved."

"Do you mean that you were framed?" Bradley asked, still not believing that anything Michael told him could possibly be true.

"It's a little more complicated than that," Michael explained. "I can't even begin to explain all of it. From my earliest years, I was a harebrained troublemaker, and I was protected by my father's immense wealth. By the time I hit thirty, in 1936, I was a complete mess and I'd already caused so much trouble for my father. Little did I know at the time, however, that things were about to become so much worse..."

CHAPTER TWENTY-SIX

September 10th, 1936...

"YOU'RE A DISGRACE," Jonathan Archer said, sitting behind his desk and peering over his spectacles at his son. "I heard about what happened the other night at the Red Cow. Must you persist in going to these drinking establishments and making a complete fool of yourself?"

"I was just having fun," Michael replied, shifting uncomfortably from one foot to the other. He couldn't hide a faint smirk. "I'm sorry about the damage. I'll pay for it."

"No, you won't," Jonathan said archly. "I have already reimbursed the landlord for the cost of the window you smashed. I also added a little extra to compensate him for the disruption, and for the possibility that people will stop frequenting the place if they fear that you might be there."

"Why would anyone do that?" Michael asked. "I'm the life and soul of the party!"

"It's not as if you *could* pay, anyway," Jonathan continued. "I understand that you neglected to show up at the mill for the role that I arranged. I had to work very hard to persuade Mr. Arbutter to give you a chance, and you couldn't even be bothered to try it for one day. Tell me, boy, do you intend to ever do an honest day's work in your life, or are you planning to merely fritter everything away?"

"I tried to get a job in the pit," Michael reminded him. "You've told them not to employ me there."

"I won't have a son of mine going down into those pits. It's too dangerous."

"I'm not entirely convinced that you -"

"There are too many accidents. You know a man who lost a leg down there, you shouldn't need reminding of the horrors of that place."

"It's hard, back-breaking work, and I want to do it," Michael said firmly. "You tell me to get a job, but you insist on choosing what jobs I'm allowed to take, and it always has to be with one of *your* companies. You tell me I should get married, but you demand the right to choose my wife. Don't you understand? I'm not rebelling against all responsibility, I'm rebelling against your incessant attempts to turn me into a copy of you!"

"There seems to be very little chance of that ever happening," Jonathan noted. "Get out of my sight. I have to go and speak to the shopkeepers about their rents. Apparently Eric Grace is offering them better terms to move to his premises. I swear, that man never stops thinking of ways to encroach upon my business!"

***

Once he'd left his father's office, Michael Archer strolled past the Red Cow, then past the Town Hall, and tried to work out what he was going to do with his day. He couldn't miss the disapproving glances that came his way from most of the people he passed, but he was used to that and the days were long gone when he'd feel even remotely bothered.

"Good morning there," he said to Walter Warden, whose expression of disdain was particularly strong as he emerged from a nearby shop. "I hope the Lord is keeping you busy."

Walter scowled at him, but Michael kept walking and didn't even look back.

By the time he passed the end of Winter Street, Michael knew exactly where he was going. He'd tried to hide his hangover from his father, but he was feeling rough and he supposed that a drink would sort his head out. Already, he could see the sign of The Butcher's Arms public house up ahead. Although he had a big evening planned, he told himself that there was no harm in having one early drink.

***

"I heard Eric Grace is buying the old music hall," Matthew 'Hoppy' Lovegood said as he sipped the foam top from his beer. "I heard he's going to turn it into a picture house."

"Who wants a picture house in Crowford?" Michael replied. "That man doesn't have any sense for business."

"A lot of people go over to Malmeston on a weekend to see the new release," Hoppy informed him. "They make a whole night of it, they have a few drinks before and then they see the picture, and then they have a few more drinks before coming home. Times are changing, Michael. I happen to think that the music hall has no future in its present state. If they put on some good talkies, they'll rake the cash in."

"My father had a chance to buy that place years ago," Michael told him, "and he said the building ought to be condemned. If Eric Grace wants to sink his money into a cesspit, then I don't see why any of us should lift a finger to stop him."

"Hey, look out there," Hoppy said, peering past him and looking at a group of women who were passing the pub. "I wouldn't mind getting to know them a little better."

Michael turned and saw that the women were crossing the road. He recognized them all immediately, although his gaze naturally fell onto Eve Marsh just as Eve happened to look over at the pub and spot him. Smiling, Michael saw that Eve instantly began to blush.

"Hang on," Hoppy said, turning around and struggling for a moment to slide the pub's window open.

"Don't do that!" Gordon barked at him from behind the bar. "You'll let all the heat out!"

"Ladies!" Hoppy shouted, waving at the women. "Do any of you fancy a drink?"

The woman laughed, but they kept walking, although Eve couldn't help looking over her shoulder. Michael offered her a slight wave, but she didn't dare respond. Still, as she turned and walked off with her friends, Michael was already thinking about the little meeting he'd arranged with her for that evening.

"I don't mind the look of their skirts," Hoppy said. "You don't think my situation would put any of them off, do you?"

Michael looked down at Hoppy's left leg, which had been amputated just above the knee a few years earlier.

"Shut that window!" Gordon shouted.

Hoppy did as he was told, before turning back to take another sip of his beer.

"Sometimes I think I should just go to that foreman and *demand* to be allowed to work in the pit," Michael muttered darkly. "My father has no right to stop me."

"No-one'll go against his wishes, though," Hoppy pointed out. "Not around here."

"Why can't he get it through his thick head that I don't want to be like him?" Michael asked. "I don't want boring office work, I want to get stuck into something physical."

"If you want to do that, you'll have to leave Crowford."

"I shouldn't have to leave my hometown to get away from my father's shadow," Michael replied, irritated by the suggestion. "I happen to like Crowford a great deal, and I have no intention of going anywhere. The old man can't control my life forever, he has to give me a break at some point. And until he does that, I suppose I might as well sit around and have some nice drinks."

"Such a hard life you lead."

"People already think the worst of me," Michael pointed out. "I might as well live down to their expectations."

"What do you think about that Eve Marsh

girl?" Hoppy asked.

"What do you mean?"

"She's a teacher at the school. She's caught my eye a few times recently, and I was thinking of maybe asking her to go dancing one night."

"You? Dancing?" Michael looked down at his friend's missing leg. "No offense, but..."

"I can make do on my sticks," Hoppy replied. "I've overheard some of those girls talking, and they can be very mean. I don't think most of them would want to go out with a guy like me, on account of my disability, but I reckon Eve's different. Do you think it'd be completely idiotic of me to have a try with her?"

"I don't think you'll get very far," Michael said, hoping to gently dissuade his friend. "You might put her in an awkward situation."

"I suppose you're right. Who wants a man who can only hop about, anyway?"

"You'll find someone," Michael told him. "There are plenty of nice girls in Crowford."

"If I didn't know better," Hoppy replied, "I'd be started to think that you have a vested interest in all this. I know some of those schoolgirls have the hots for you, especially the shy ones, but they don't really strike me as your type. You don't have the hots for Ms. Marsh, do you?"

"Of course not," Michael said, before taking a long swig from his pint. "Now let's stop talking about daft things and get out of here."

"You don't want another drink? It's not like we've got anywhere to rush off to."

"Speak for yourself," Michael told him, as he looked at the clock on the wall. "I can't get too drunk today. There's somewhere I have to be later."

CHAPTER TWENTY-SEVEN

HOURS LATER, STOPPING OUTSIDE the school building, Michael looked up at the door. He was carrying a single red rose, and he could feel a knot of apprehension in the pit of his belly. He'd met Eve for private little encounters several times already, but he was finally going to tell her how he really felt; he was finally going to tell her that he wanted, one day, to make her his wife.

After heading up the steps, he tried to open the door, only to find that it was locked. He wasn't particularly surprised, but – as he turned and looked back across the empty yard – he realized that he was a good half an hour early. The thought of hanging around in the cold for thirty minutes wasn't particularly appealing, so of course naturally his thoughts turned to the Crowford Farrier, a public house just a short walk away. He'd been good all day, only drinking one pint, but now he supposed that there was no harm in having one more while he waited, just to provide a little extra courage.

He began to hurry down the steps, only to hesitate as he looked down at the rose in his hands. The Crowford Farrier could be a rough place, even on a cold Thursday night, and the last thing he wanted was for the rose to get crushed. Spotting a gap behind one of the pillars, he headed over and tucked the rose out of sight, before setting off down the steps and across the yard.

Stopping suddenly, he looked to his left.

He waited, convinced that he'd heard a scuffing sound, but there was no sign of anyone. Still, he headed over to the corner of the building and looked round, just to be certain.

"Anyone there?" he called out. "Eve?"

He waited a moment longer, and then he turned and hurried across the yard. He supposed that he just had time for a quick pint, and then he could get back to the school and be ready to surprise Eve.

***

Stumbling slightly as he made his way along the alley, Michael bumped against the wall and stopped to steady himself. He'd only gone for one pint, but somehow that had become three and now he was twenty minutes late for his meeting with Eve. He hated himself for having been so easily distracted, but at the same time it hadn't been his fault that he'd bumped into so many people he knew.

He'd taken a mint before leaving the pub, and he hoped that would disguise any smell of alcohol.

Once he reached the schoolyard, he headed straight to the front of the main building and hurried up the steps. As he'd expected, the front door was now open, and he felt a flicker of joy as he realized that Eve would be waiting for him inside. He stepped through into the hallway and looked around, and he listened for any sign of her. Deep down, he felt guilty for keeping her waiting, but he was determined to help her get warm. And then, remembering the rose, he stepped back outside and reached behind the pillar.

To his surprise, he found that the rose was gone.

"Huh," he muttered, realizing that Eve must have found the rose and taken it inside. That made the whole thing slightly less romantic, but he hoped that it might at least have made up for his tardiness.

Once he was back inside, he took a look along the corridors, and then he made his way upstairs. In his mind's eye, he was already imagining Eve waiting for him, and he began to rehearse what he was going to say to her.

"Eve Marsh," he thought to himself as he walked toward the set of double doors, "one day I'm going to make you an honest woman. Next year, I promise. I just need to get a few things sorted out first."

Reaching the doors, he hesitated.

"I'm sorry I made you call me Adam," he imagined himself telling her, "but I didn't want you to know who I really am. I should tell you the truth, though, so here goes. I'm Michael Archer. Yes, *that* family. Jonathan Archer is my father. I know I have a bad reputation, but I want you to know that none of it's true. Well, most of it's not, anyway, and..."

He paused for a moment longer, and finally he realized something that he found rather shocking, something that went against all his instincts.

"I'll take a job with my father's company," he was going to tell her. "I've resisted it for so long, but you deserve someone who'll look after you properly. I'll go to the old man tomorrow and I'll tell him. He'll be happy, he'll think he's won, but all that matters is me looking after you. And after the kids we're going to have one day, too. I'll do all of that for you, Eve. I'm going to make you the happiest woman in the whole goddamn world."

With that, he took a deep breath and pushed the doors open, stepping into the room only to stop as soon as he saw a bloodied figure slumped on the floor.

He stared at her, and for a moment he was unable to process what was happening.

"Eve?" he said cautiously, taking a step toward her before stopping as he saw the red rose resting on the floor nearby. "Eve, are you..."

He hesitated for a moment, and then he hurried over and dropped to his knees. He reached out to touch her, and then he froze again as he saw that the back of her dress was covered in blood. The fabric was torn in several places, and when he looked up at the back of her neck he saw another thick wound.

"Eve?"

He rolled her onto her back, and then he let out a horrified gasp as he saw her dead eyes staring up toward the ceiling. A moment later, spotting a knife nearby, he reached out and picked it up. In the moonlight, the blood-stained blade briefly glinted, and Michael let the knife fall from his hand as he leaned over Eve and began to shake her.

"Eve, it's me!" he shouted. "Eve, say something!"

He checked in vain for a pulse.

"I'm sorry I was late," he told her, as tears ran down his face. "I was going to tell you everything, I was going to tell you that I'm going to ask you to marry me some day, Eve. Can you hear me? Please, if there's still some part of you in there, let me know that you can hear me."

Even as he shook her some more, he knew that he was too late, and finally he gathered Eve's lifeless body up into his arms and got to his feet. Locked in some kind of trance-like state, he turned and began to carry her out of the room. She felt so light in his arms, as if he could feel that her soul was no longer in her body, and as he reached the top of the stairs Michael felt more tears running down his face.

"I'm going to save you," he whispered, although he could hear the shock in his own voice. "I don't know how, but I'm going to find a doctor and I'm going to make him fix you up good. You've just got to hang on in there, Eve, do you hear me? You've got to be strong for a little while longer, that's all, and then everything's going to be okay."

He carried Eve out of the school, out into the cold air of the schoolyard. He knew not to look down at her, because he knew that looking down at her would mean having to acknowledge what had happened, so he simply focused on the path ahead as he made his way along the alley. He almost tripped, but finally he emerged from the alley and began to carry Eve along London Road. The urge to look at her pretty face was getting stronger, but so too was the need to deny reality for a little while longer.

Finally, reaching Crowford Police Station,

he stopped outside and stared at the front door. He could see someone working at the desk, and after a moment the man glanced up.

A moment later, Sergeant Cooper emerged from the station and began to make his way toward Michael, only to slow as he began to realize what he was holding in his arms.

"Michael Archer," Cooper said cautiously, "what are you doing there? What's going on?"

He peered at Eve's lifeless body.

"Who's that you're carrying?" he asked. "Michael, you need to start talking right now!"

"She needs help," Michael replied, and now tears were streaming down his face. "Someone did this to her. She needs a doctor, do you understand? Hurry, man, while there's still time. You have to fetch help!"

CHAPTER TWENTY-EIGHT

"AND THAT'S WHAT THE official version of events will record?" Jonathan Archer whispered as he stood with Sergeant Allison in a corridor at the police station. "That she was found at the school?"

"I'll make sure that a couple of my men are sent over first thing," Allison replied. "There'll be no record of him having brought her here, but Jonathan..."

His voice trailed off.

"I know," Jonathan replied, his voice heavy with regret. "He's caused trouble in the past, but he's never done anything as bad as this."

"He swears he didn't kill her."

"And do you believe him?"

"Well, I mean..." Allison hesitated for a moment. "He gave us a statement. He was quite convincing, although the story sounded rather unlikely. There's also the fact that we found a knife at the scene. Michael claims to have held it, and I have no doubt that we'll find his fingerprints on the handle."

"It's okay, man," Jonathan continued, "you don't have to finish that sentence. We both know how this looks, and I'm long past the stage of giving my son the benefit of the doubt. I'm just very grateful to you for coming to me and giving me a chance to help put this right. I wouldn't want word getting out that..."

He paused, and then he reached into his pocket and pulled out an envelope, which he handed to Allison.

"It's all there," he told him, "you can count it if you want. I won't be offended."

"I wouldn't dream of counting it, Sir," Allison replied, already pocketing the money. "I should tell you, though, that there's only so much I can do. Eve Marsh was a popular young woman in this town. If Michael ever does anything like this again... There's only so much that can get swept under the rug, is all I'm saying. Jonathan, we've known one another for a long time, and I like to think that I can speak my mind to you. You need to get that boy under control!"

"I know," Jonathan replied, with a heavy heart. "One way or another."

***

"What the hell do you think you're doing out here?" Jonathan asked a few hours later, as he stood in front of the town hall and saw Michael slumped on the ground. "Have you no shame?"

"He was wailing as if he was in pain," a woman said, watching from a safe distance. "He can't be drunk *this* early in the morning, can he? It's barely even eight o'clock!"

"Get up," Jonathan said, stepping over to Michael and trying to haul him to his feet. "Come on, boy, you mustn't do this in broad daylight. Let's get you to my office!"

"I didn't touch her," Michael said, slurring his words so badly that they barely made sense at all. Looking up at his father, he struggled to focus. "You have to believe me."

"I don't believe anything you tell me anymore," Jonathan replied. "I'm your father and I'm ordering you to get up at once!" He glanced around and saw that a growing crowd was gathering. "Michael," he continued, lowering his voice a little, "for the love of all that's holy, you're embarrassing us both!"

Michael tried to stand, only to immediately slump back down.

"I shall have to send for some men to help,"

Jonathan muttered under his breath, before turning to the people who were watching. "Do you lot have nothing better to do with your days? Are you all just going to stand there, gawping at a man who has had too much to drink? You should all be ashamed of yourselves!"

The crowd began to disperse, until Jonathan saw one particular man standing near the back. This man was the person he least wanted to encounter on that cold Friday morning.

"Oh dear," Eric Grace said, stepping forward with a big smile on his face as he looked down at Michael, who had slipped back into unconsciousness. "Your son appears to have had rather a tough time of late. Would you like me to arrange for someone to come and carry him into your office for you?"

"I am perfectly capable of having that done, Eric," Jonathan muttered darkly. "Thank you, all the same, for the offer."

"You know," Eric continued, "I heard something very troubling just now, before I came into town. I heard that a young teacher was found brutally murdered at the school up near London Road. Apparently the place has been sealed off while the police carry out their investigation."

"I'm sorry," Jonathan replied, "but I don't have time to -"

"I also heard that your boy Michael was at

the police station for several hours during the night, assisting with that investigation. I know you probably won't want to hear this, Jonathan, but there are whispers going around town that Michael might have had something to do with the girl's death."

"That's outrageous!" Jonathan snapped. "I can well imagine who is behind those rumors!"

"You're not accusing me again, are you?"

"I know you better than you realize, Eric," Jonathan sneered. "Let's cut to the chase. Whenever you think you have some dirt on me, you seek to leverage that position. What is it that you want this time?"

"I'm merely an old friend who happened to be passing," Eric replied. "We *were* friends once, Jonathan. Or don't you remember?"

"That was a very long time ago," Jonathan pointed out. "We were children."

"And look at us now. Between us, we own almost the entire town, although lately I seem to have been picking up a few extra properties. I don't want to brag, Jonathan, but I fancy that I perhaps have overtaken you now as the preeminent landlord in Crowford. And at least my girls aren't out getting drunk every night and causing trouble. They were raised to behave themselves."

"Excuse me," Jonathan replied, turning to head back to his office so that he could summon help, "I have to attend to my son."

"I'm buying the music hall," Eric added.

Jonathan stopped and turned back to him.

"The deal should go through today," Eric continued. "Don't even think to try to stop it, because you can't. I think it's time for the movies to come to Crowford, so I'm going to turn the hall into a picture palace. I know that's a rather risky proposition, but I can see it succeeding. Movies are the future, Jonathan. Isn't that exciting?" He paused. "Of course, it would have a better chance if I could also buy that revolting hotel next door and do something about its revolting appearance."

"I'm not selling the Grand!" Jonathan snapped angrily. "I've told you that before!"

"You have indeed," Eric replied, "but I was thinking that you might have changed your mind. After all, it would be a terrible shame if any weight were to be put behind the rumors of your son's involvement in last night's awful murder."

"Are you blackmailing me again?" Jonathan asked.

"I'm suggesting a course of action that might be beneficial to both of us. I'll buy the Grand from you and either knock it down or have it heavily renovated, and you won't have to worry about people gossiping that your dear son is a common murderer. You'd like that, wouldn't you?"

"You're despicable!" Jonathan snapped. "How long do you think you can keep doing this to me?"

"For as long as it takes," Eric replied. "I'm not done building my little empire up just yet."

Before Jonathan could reply, he heard a sudden retching sound, and he turned to see that Michael was vomiting onto the grass. A moment later a figure stopped nearby, and Jonathan saw that one of Michael's friends had arrived.

"You there!" he barked at the man. "You know my son, do you not? Can you gather a few sturdy fellows and have them come to carry him inside?"

"Me?" Hoppy replied, looking down at Michael for a moment. "I'm sorry, I'm in too much of a rush. Besides, I'm not sure that we're friends anymore, not after what I heard about..."

His voice trailed off, and then he turned and hurried away, leaning heavily on his sticks.

"I'm sure you'll manage perfectly well," Eric said as he stepped past Jonathan and patted his former friend on the back. "I have to go, I'm afraid. I'm meeting the gentlemen who own the dance hall, to finalize our deal. Oh, and I'll have my men draw up a contract for the sale of the Grand. I know you just told me that you won't sell it but, well, I have a rather funny feeling that you'll soon change your mind."

With that, he walked away, leaving Jonathan standing all alone and watching as Michael continued to vomit.

"I'm going to lose it all, aren't I?" Jonathan whispered, as a cold wind blew along the street. "I'm going to lose every penny, and that wretched Eric Grace is going to get it all. And the worst part is that there is absolutely nothing I can do to change that fact."

CHAPTER TWENTY-NINE

May, 1988...

"MY FATHER LIVED FOR another decade after that awful day," Michael said, as he and Bradley sat in the kitchen of the icy little cottage. "It was just long enough for him to see his empire getting torn down, piece by piece. His sacrifice didn't even work, because gossip still spread. I was blamed for every bad thing that ever happened in Crowford, and finally I had no choice but to leave."

"So who *did* kill Eve Marsh?" Bradley asked cautiously. "Assuming that I believe your version, which I'm not saying that I do."

"I suppose we'll never find out," Michael replied. "Believe me, I've tried to come up with an answer. The truth is that most likely it was an opportunistic crime, carried out perhaps by someone who was just passing through the town. If I had been on time for the meeting with Eve, if I hadn't allowed myself to get delayed in that pub, most likely nothing bad would have happened. In that sense, at least, I suppose you could argue that I did indeed kill the woman I loved. I certainly bear some responsibility for her death."

"But you didn't actually do it?"

"It's alright," Michael muttered, "I don't expect or require you to believe me. Old man Grace died about ten years after my father, and as far as I know the empire of Crowford passed into the hands of his two daughters. I remember them, they were prim and proper little things. One of them even had a little crush on me for a while. It's strange how things work out, isn't it? If only I had been a better person, a better son, my father's control of the town would have been passed down to me and the Graces would be nothing but a footnote in Crowford's history. As I said to you earlier, however, I don't want to be considered a victim. There's only one victim, and that's Eve. I only wish that I had died in her place. She deserved a full and happy life."

Bradley waited for Michael to continue, but he realized after a moment that the old man seemed lost in his memories.

"I saw Eve today," Bradley said finally.

"What are you talking about?"

"She's still there," Bradley continued. "I know how this sounds, but it's true, I swear! She was in the big hall in the old school building, and she was screaming. She's written your name all over the walls. Well, not *your* name exactly, she's written the name Adam. She never knew who you really were, did she?"

"I didn't get the chance to tell her. I wanted to protect her."

"I think she wants something," Bradley explained. "I don't know if it's revenge, or if she's just really sad, but I came here tonight because I thought I could record you, as a ghost, confessing to everything. I thought that might help her."

"You're just a child," Michael muttered, getting to his feet and limping over to the counter. "This isn't some kind of adventure. It's a tragedy, and nothing can change that."

"Her ghost -"

"Ghosts don't exist!" he snapped, turning to him. "They *can't* exist, and do you know why? Because if they do, that means that my dear, darling Eve has been in that school all this time, for more than fifty years. It means that she's been trapped there, alone and suffering, wondering why I never went back to see her. I can't even begin to consider that possibility, because I can't comprehend such a vast amount of pain." He paused, with tears in his eyes. "No," he continued, "there's no ghost. Eve is gone. Her soul died with her body on that awful night more than half a decade ago, and that was the end of it."

"You're wrong," Bradley replied. "We almost got proof that she's real and -"

"No!" Michael shouted angrily, slamming his fist against the counter. "Why would you come all this way just to tell me something so awful?"

"Because it's the truth," Bradley said, terrified but forcing himself to remain seated. "Are you sure you don't want to record a message for her? I don't know if it would work, I'm just guessing, but isn't it at least worth a try?"

"You're just a child!" Michael yelled, storming over to him.

Bradley get to his feet and backed into the corner.

"You don't understand anything!" Michael sneered. "Do you seriously think that what happened all those years ago can be condensed into the form of a foolish little ghost story?"

"I -"

"Never!" Michael snarled, grabbing Bradley by the collar and lifting him up, pinning him against the wall with almost superhuman strength. "She's dead and she's gone and nothing can ever be done to change that, do you hear me? You should never have come here with your sniveling little stories, you pathetic piece of -"

"Get away from my son!"

Suddenly Debbie rushed into the room and grabbed Michael, pulling him away from Bradley and then shoving him across the room with such force that the old man tripped and fell. Crying out in pain as he landed, Michael rolled onto his side and struggled for a moment to get his breath back.

"What are you doing here?" Debbie gasped, dropping to her knees and frantically checking to see whether Bradley was alright. "Are you hurt?"

Bradley shook his head, but he was struggling to hold back tears.

Debbie turned and looked over at Michael, who had managed to pull himself up and was leaning his back against one of the counters.

"Who..." Debbie began, but then she fell silent as she saw Michael's face.

"It's him," Bradley told her. "It's Michael Archer, he's not dead."

"That's impossible," Debbie replied, momentarily too shocked to move. "It can't be him. Please, tell me it isn't him."

Michael let out a grunt of pain as he again tried to stand.

"Move," Debbie said suddenly, turning Bradley around and pushing him out of the room. "I don't know what's going on, but we're getting out of here."

"Mum -"

"I said, *move!*"

She forced Bradley all the way out of the farmhouse. Once they were standing in the mud, she stopped and looked back at the door, and they both heard the sound of Michael still scrabbling about on the floor, still desperately trying to stand.

"I talked to him," Bradley explained. "He told me what really happened."

"Michael Archer's dead," Debbie replied. "Everyone knows that."

"He just pretended to be dead so he could find out what people would say about him," Bradley continued. "He says that it was all lies, and that he never really did anything wrong. He said -"

"No!" Debbie snapped, turning to him. "Michael Archer was a monster."

"But -"

"And he's dead, Bradley!" she added, cutting him off again. "I don't know what you saw in there, but -"

"You saw him too!"

"No!" Grabbing his hand, she forced him to follow her across the muddy ground, heading back toward the road. "We're going home," she continued, her voice filled with panic. "I don't want any more talk of Michael Archer or of things that happened before either of us had even been born. Do you understand? And you absolutely are not to say anything like that to your grandmother!"

"But I really talked to him," Bradley complained. "You saw him too, you pushed him away. Mum, he told me that -"

"Just shut up!" she yelled, stopping and turning to him. "Bradley," she continued breathlessly, "I'm begging you, stop this right now. It's getting so bad, you're even making me start seeing things. I knew I'd find you here. As soon as I realized you were missing, and I saw that you'd been going through my papers, I knew exactly what you were up to. It's got to stop, Bradley. I don't blame you, not really. I blame your father, he's obviously been letting you read those awful comics and watch those awful films, and now you don't even know what's real and what's just fantasy. But it has to stop. After everything you've done today, I can't just stand by and let you perpetuate this nonsense."

"Everything I've told you is true," he replied, with tears in his eyes. "I can prove it, too. Why won't you believe me?"

"Enough with the proof talk," she said, shaking her head. "Bradley, you -"

Before she could finish, she spotted movement in the distance. The lights were still on in the farmhouse, and a figure had limped into the open doorway. Debbie felt a shudder past through her chest as she saw the figure standing still, and she worried that somehow – despite the darkness all around – the figure could see her and Bradley. For a moment, she considered the possibility that this was the man who she'd been told, just a few hours earlier, was her biological father.

"Move," she said finally, grabbing Bradley's hand again and forcing him to continue to march to the stone wall, and to the car parked on the other side. "I don't know what's going on out here, but we're going home!"

CHAPTER THIRTY

AS THE CAR REACHED the outskirts of Crowford, Bradley sat silently in the back seat and looked down at the tape recorder. He and his mother hadn't spoken during the drive back, and Bradley had been trying to figure out how he was ever going to make anyone believe him.

"So that old man at the farmhouse," Debbie said finally, keeping her eyes fixed on the empty road ahead. "You know he can't have been Michael Archer, right?"

"He was, Mum."

"No, he wasn't. Obviously some hobo has moved into Archer's old cottage and -"

"It was him!"

"Will you be quiet and let me explain?" she continued. "You've been living in a fantasy, Bradley, and you need a dose of reality. Obviously that man, whoever he was, has some kind of delusion in his head, he thinks he's Michael Archer. It's understandable that you got confused, but really, it wasn't him. There are a lot of very strange people in this world, and you can't always take what they say at face value."

She slowed the car at a set of emergency traffic lights, where some workers were carrying out late-night repairs to the road. For a moment, she simply drummed her fingertips against the steering wheel. She knew she needed to find a way to get through to her son, but she couldn't quite come up with the right words.

"It can't have been him," she added.

"I can prove it," Bradley replied, as he started rewinding the tape. "He didn't know it, but while he was talking to me, I managed to record him."

"Bradley -"

"Just listen, Mum!"

He hit the button to start playing the tape, and as the hissing sound began he waited to hear the old man's voice again.

"Careful with accusations like that," Michael's voice said a moment later, sounding a little cracked on the recording. "You don't want to believe everything you read in the Crowford Gazette."

"Everyone knows you did it," Bradley's voice replied.

"And everyone's wrong!" Michael said firmly, before collapsing into a brief coughing fit.

"Turn that off," Debbie said, getting frustrated as the traffic light ahead remained red.

"You've no idea, young man," Michael continued on the tape, "of the amount of pure horseshit that's been talked about me over the years. Do you know who I am? Who I *really* am, I mean. Do you know about my family, about how the Archers once owned half of Crowford?"

"Turn that off!" Debbie snapped angrily. "Don't make me tell you again!"

"Wait," Bradley said, fast-forwarding for a few seconds, "there's a better part where he explains it more."

"Bradley, this is ridiculous," she muttered, as the light remained red. "Are these lights even working?"

"- else in Crowford just believed what they wanted to believe," Michael's voice said on the tape as Bradley started it up again. "Instead of accepting that various people had done bad things, they lumped all the sins of the town onto me."

"Turn it off!" Debbie shouted, looking back at Bradley.

She reached out to grab the recorder, but he managed to keep it out of her hands. He pressed the button to stop the recording, but – shocked by his mother's reaction – he could only stare at her.

"I don't want to ever hear the name Michael Archer again," she told him, "and that's my final word on the matter." She paused, out of breath, and a moment later she turned to look ahead once more. After a couple of seconds, the light switched to green, but Debbie didn't immediately start driving again.

Bradley waited, and then as he glanced out the window he saw the old school building in the distance, just about visible in the darkness behind a row of terraced houses. In that instant, he thought of Eve Marsh's ghost still haunting the cold, empty corridors, and he wondered how she'd react if she knew the truth about Michael Archer. After a moment, he looked down at the recorder again.

In the driver's seat, Debbie was trying to pull herself together. She knew she shouldn't really be driving at all, but they were so close to home now. She stared at the green light and told herself to just take it slowly and drive back to the house, but her hands were starting to shake. Although she'd assumed at first that she was simply upset about all the craziness that had happened during the day, now she was worried that she might be on the verge of fainting, that her illness was trying to assert itself again.

"Give me a moment," she murmured,

reaching up and wiping cold sweat from her face. "Damn it, not now."

For a few seconds, she thought back to the sight of the old man in the farmhouse. He couldn't have been Michael Archer, of course; she knew that Michael Archer was dead, and she was glad of that fact. A long time had passed since she'd seen a picture of Michael, so it was hard for her to be sure, but she figured that the man in the farmhouse was just some random man. In that case, she was hugely relieved that she'd managed to get to Bradley before anything truly bad had happened.

The light ahead turned amber, then red again. Taking a deep breath, Debbie told herself that she'd drive as soon as the light turned back to green, and that she just had to regain her composure. She opened her mouth to tell Bradley that everything was going to be okay, but she couldn't quite manage to get the words out. Instead, she focused on gripping the wheel properly, and on running through the turns she'd have to take in order to get back to the right street. She felt as if some kind of fog was starting to fill her mind.

The light turned green again.

She hesitated.

Suddenly she heard a clicking sound from the back seat, and then one of the doors opened.

"Bradley," she stammered, "what -"

"I have to let her hear it!" he gasped, already

racing away from the car. "She has to know the truth!"

"Are you kidding me?" Debbie snapped, unfastening her seat belt and quickly clambering out of the car, just as she saw Bradley disappearing along a nearby street. "Bradley!" she shouted. "Get back here!"

She waited, but he was gone and a moment later she too saw the old school in the distance. Sighing, she briefly considered running after her son, but then she climbed back into the car. She knew exactly where he was going, so with a growing sense of frustration and anger she put the car in gear and began to drive, even as the light turned back to red.

"Hey!" one of the workmen yelled as she drove past.

"Sorry," she muttered under her breath, but she was already focused on the road ahead.

All thought of her illness was suddenly pushed to the back of her mind as she thought of Bradley running to the school, and she was furious with herself for not having realized that he might try to pull another stunt. Bradley had always been a good boy, perhaps a little nervous at times, but something had clearly changed in him and she couldn't help thinking that it was her fault. She'd always told herself with pride that her son was strong and resilient, but now she was starting to realize that he was really struggling.

A couple of minutes later, as she parked outside the school's main gate, Debbie realized that she was going to have to find a way to make Bradley accept the truth. Including the one thing that they both knew, and that they'd both been trying to ignore.

She was going to have to be honest with him about her illness.

Wincing as she stepped out of the car, she hurried past the gate and made her way toward the old building. She felt increasingly weak, but nothing could stop her going after her son and she soon reached the field. She stumbled a little as she rushed across the grass, and finally she got to the old yard. She could see that the old school's doors were open at the front, and she knew that meant that Bradley must have gone inside. Still, she slowed a little as she got closer to the building, and finally she stopped at the bottom of the steps.

Looking up at the tall, imposing building, she felt as if some presence was lingering in the air all around, warning her to stay back. As she looked at the highest windows she couldn't help but wonder whether she might actually see a ghostly face staring back down. She quickly told herself, however, that such thoughts were foolish. She knew, she'd *always* known, that ghosts were not real.

And then, suddenly, she heard Bradley cry out.

CHAPTER THIRTY-ONE

"BRADLEY!" DEBBIE SHOUTED, rushing into the school's hallway and then stopping as she heard a faint bumping sound coming from somewhere upstairs. "I'm coming!"

Racing up to the top floor, she followed the sound of what seemed to be a struggle, and finally she reached the old main hall. To her shock, she saw that Bradley was struggling with a figure, and after a moment the tape recorder fell to the ground and slid over to the far wall. Immediately, the figure threw Bradley aside and raced after the recorder, scooping it up before turning and seeing Debbie.

"Lou?" she said. "What the hell are *you* doing here?"

"Stopping your kid making a big mistake, by the looks of things," he said breathlessly. "He just walked in here and started playing this stupid thing out loud!"

"She has to hear what he said!" Bradley shouted, rushing over to Lou and trying to grab the machine, only to get pushed away. "She has to know the truth! In his own words!"

He tried again to grab the recorder. This time Lou was firmer, pushing him so hard that he sent Bradley tumbling down to the floor.

"Don't touch my son!" Debbie snapped, rushing over and helping Bradley up. "Lou, that happens to be my tape recorder, so I think you need to give it back to me right now."

"You're lucky I was here!" Lou told her, still a little out of breath from all the exertion. "Do you really think it's safe for the boy to be here in the middle of the night? Quite apart from the possibility of someone attacking him, the building isn't exactly safe. I know you're going through a tough time at the moment, Debbie, but there's no excuse for bad parenting. Sorry, Debbie, but it appears that you've really taken your eye off the ball. The kid's a mess."

"Just shut up and give me the recorder!" she said firmly. "What *are* you doing here, anyway?"

"He was taking photos," Bradley explained.

"The kid's a fantasist," Lou sneered. "He's trouble. I can tell that just from looking at him."

"He was taking photos of the walls," Bradley continued.

"Lou?" Debbie said cautiously, as she saw that there was indeed a camera hanging from a cord around her former boss's neck. "It's almost midnight. What are you doing wandering around in here?"

"Someone asked me to come and check the place out before it gets knocked down," he replied a little evasively. "I'm simply taking some photos for the historical record. Soon this old dump will be gone, and rightly or wrongly it's a part of the Crowford's past. Consider me a founding member of the Crowford Historical Society." He raised his camera and took a picture of Debbie and Bradley, causing the flash to briefly light the room. "There, now *your* ugly mugs'll also be included for posterity. You're welcome."

"Yeah, I don't buy that for one second," Debbie said as she saw the name Adam scratched into the walls. As she looked around, she felt a chill in her bones. "Who did all of this?" she continued. "You can almost feel the sorrow and the sadness in the air."

"It was her," Bradley said. "It was the ghost of Eve Marsh. She's been here all this time."

Debbie turned to him.

"Sweetheart, you have to know that isn't true," she told him. "A place can be sad and creepy without there having to be anything supernatural going on. I think you're just struggling to explain things that you're too young to understand."

Before Bradley could reply, he heard the sound of the tape recorder starting to play again.

"- and I know that everyone thinks I killed her," Michael's voice said, cracking as the tape ran in Lou's hands. "I told them what really happened, that she was dead by the time I arrived, but no-one believed me. Or they didn't *want* to believe me. I should have pushed harder to make them uncover the truth, but in all honesty I was just too heartbroken. After Eve died, I got a lot worse. I was drinking all day, every day in an attempt to blot out the pain."

"Who *is* this?" Lou asked, looking over at Bradley. "Who's on the tape, boy?"

"It's Michael Archer," Bradley replied.

"How? The man's dead. Where did you get this?"

"He's not dead," Bradley explained. "I met him tonight."

"That's simply impossible," Lou told him, as the recording continued. "Come on, be honest with me, where did you *really* get this recording from? It's obvious that someone interviewed him while he was still alive, but when? And why?"

"We're getting out of here," Debbie said, taking Bradley's hand and trying to lead him toward the door. "Come on, it's late and we have to get home."

"There she is!" Bradley yelled, pointing past Lou.

Debbie turned, but she saw nothing.

"She was right there!" Bradley continued, as Lou also turned to look. "It was only for a second, but the ghost of Eve Marsh was standing behind him!"

"What are you talking about?" Lou muttered. "You're seeing things, boy."

"There's not a day goes by that I don't think about her," Michael's voice was saying on the tape. "If I'd just been there on time, none of this would have happened and we'd have had a happy life together. I was willing to settle down for her. I was willing to give up everything, I was even going to grovel to my father and agree to take a job in his stupid office. There was nothing I wouldn't have done for Eve. Except, apparently, show up on time to meet her."

"I know you don't believe me," Bradley said, looking up at Debbie, "but I'm not a liar. She was right behind him."

Debbie stared at the space behind Lou, but she still saw no sign of any ghostly figure.

"We have to go," she said finally, as she began to force her son toward the door. "This has been a long day, and I need to get you home."

"Wait a minute!" Lou called after them. "I need to know where this tape came from! You can't just turn up with something like this and then not explain. I need to know where you got it, and if there are any other copies! There *aren't* any other copies, are there? Just tell me that, and then you can be on your way."

"Ignore him," Debbie muttered. "Bradley, when we get home we're going to have to have a proper talk about the importance of -"

Suddenly Lou cried out. Debbie and Bradley both turned to see that some invisible force seemed to be pulling him back, and after a moment the tape recorder fell from his hands and hit the floor hard. Lou was shaking violently and his eyes were open wide as he coughed and spluttered, but he was unable to get a word out as he slowly began to tilt his head back.

"What's happening to him?" Debbie whispered.

"It's her," Bradley replied. "It has to be."

"I think he's having some kind of heart attack," Debbie said, letting go of Bradley's hand and hurrying back across the room. "Or a stroke. Lou, it's okay, I'm going to get you a -"

In that instant, she froze as she saw the truth.

She blinked, convinced that she must be imagining things, but Eve Marsh was visible in the darkness now, standing right behind Lou and pressing her hands against the sides of his head. Her fingertips were digging into his scalp, and after a moment she began to drag her fingers straight down through his face, causing a loud scratching sound to ring out across the room.

"No," Debbie whispered, as she stared at the dead woman's eyes, "this can't be real..."

"Help me..." Lou gasped, finally managing to speak as blood began to run from the cuts on his face. "Please, you have to..."

Eve's ghost briefly faded from sight, before returning more clearly than before.

"Mum?" Bradley said cautiously, grabbing Debbie's hand from behind and trying to pull her toward the door. "I think maybe we should go now."

"This can't be happening," Debbie stammered, taking a step forward and then – as her legs buckled – dropping to her knees. For a moment, she could only stare in horror at the sight of the dead woman who was still slowly slicing her hands through Lou's body.

"Please," Lou gasped, "get this bitch off me! You have to -"

Before he could say another word, Eve reached up and grabbed his head, and then she broke his neck before letting his corpse thud down against the wooden floor.

"She's real," Debbie whispered, as Eve's spectral face was reflected in her eyes. "Ghosts are real."

CHAPTER THIRTY-TWO

"MUM," BRADLEY SAID CAUTIOUSLY, stepping up behind Debbie and tugging once again on her arm. His eyes were still fixed on the sight of Eve Marsh, who was just about visible as she towered over Lou's corpse. "Hey, Mum, I think maybe we should get out of here. She looks angry."

Barely even hearing her son's words, Debbie stared at the ghostly vision. She was seeing a dead woman, something that went completely against her comprehension of reality. Eve was there and not there at the same time, ephemeral and constantly phasing in and out of sight. For a few seconds, she seemed almost to be dissolving into nothing, but then some other force – sheer willpower, perhaps - pulled her back and made her more solid for a moment, before the process repeated again and again. Her eyes were filled with the fury of deep, cold death.

After a few seconds, Eve finally faded from view, and Debbie blinked a couple of times as she looked down at Lou.

"Is he..."

"I think he's dead, Mum," Bradley explained, looking around in case Eve appeared again. "I hoped that hearing Michael's voice would calm Eve down and make her happy, but I think it made her mad instead." He pulled on her arm again. "Mum, please, can we get out of here? I'm don't have another plan."

Debbie hesitated, before getting to her feet. She, too, was looking around for any further sign of Eve, but after a few seconds she grabbed Bradley's hand.

"Come on," she said as she led him toward the open doorway. "Whatever's going on here tonight, we can figure it out once we're safely at -"

Suddenly the doors slammed shut. Debbie ran forward and tried to pull them open again, but some hidden force was holding them firmly in place.

"They won't budge!" she muttered, trying not to panic as she tried the doors over and over. "I don't get it!"

Bradley turned and looked across the room. In the moonlight, he could barely see a thing, but after a moment he spotted movement at the far end of the hall as a figure briefly came into view.

"She's still here," he said, stepping back against the door.

"Bradley, I need you to help me with this," Debbie said, trying the door yet again. "There has to be a way out of here."

Bradley hesitated, before rushing over toward the spot where Lou's body had fallen. Trying not to look at the dead man, he dropped to his knees and picked up the recorder, only to find that it had landed badly and that part of the casing had come loose.

"No," he whispered as he tried in vain to get the tape to play again, "come on, if I can find the right part of the recording, it might still work. She just needs to know that he still loves her after all these years, that he hasn't forgotten her."

He looked over his shoulder, and to his horror he saw the ghost of Eve Marsh stepping up behind his mother.

"Mum, watch out!" he yelled.

Debbie spun around, and in that moment Eve vanished.

"She's not going to let us go," Bradley said, returning his focus to the recorder as he tried to figure out a way to get the buttons to work again. "Those doors locked on us before, Mum, and they only opened when Mr. Kepper tried them from the outside. I don't think we can break our way out of here, so we're going to have to try my original plan."

He finally managed to push one of the buttons. The tape began to play, but a scrunching sound immediately rang out and Bradley saw to his horror that the tape itself was ribboning out from the cassette.

"No!" he gasped, but he was too late. He pulled the tape out and began to try to wind it all back into place by hand, but he could already see that parts of the tape had been badly crunched.

"Get away from him!" Debbie screamed, suddenly rushing over to Bradley. "Leave him -"

Before she could finish, she was sent crashing into the far wall. She slumped down against the floor and let out a gasp of pain, and then she looked up just in time to see that Eve's ghostly figure was standing directly behind Bradley as he continued to try to fix the tape.

"Leave him alone," Debbie gasped, somehow managing to sit up despite the pain. "He never did anything to you!"

Slowly, Eve reached out and placed a hand on the side of Bradley's face.

"Stop!" Debbie shouted, struggling to her feet and limping toward them both. "You have to -"

In a flash, she was sent smashing into another wall. This time her head hit the plaster hard, and she was barely conscious by the time she fell to the floor. Someone managing to stay awake, she hauled herself up and looked over her shoulder just in time to see that Eve was cradling Bradley's head in her hands, holding him tight.

"Mum," Bradley gasped, dropping the recorder and looking up into Eve's eyes, "help me..."

Eve snarled as she leaned closer to Bradley, and she slowly began to force her fingertips into the sides of his face.

"No!" Debbie yelled, limping toward them. "Take me! Don't hurt him! Please, you can't hurt him, he's only a child! If you have to take someone, then take me!"

Slipping, she dropped to the floor. When she tried to get back up, she found that she was far too weak, as if her injuries and her illness were conspiring to hold her down. Her vision was starting to get a little blurred again, and for a moment she could barely even remember where she was or how she'd ended up there. Finally, however, she forced herself to focus on the fact that her son needed help.

"Bradley," she groaned.

"Mum, help me!" Bradley cried out, as Eve began to drag her fingertips down through his cheeks. "Stop!"

"Leave him alone, you bitch!" Debbie

shouted. "Do you hear me? Just because you're miserable, that doesn't mean you have the right to hurt other people! I'm sure you were wronged, I'm sure you want to get your revenge on everyone who ruined your life, but my son is not one of those people!" She hesitated, but Eve appeared not to have even heard her words. "Stop!" Debbie screamed. "You can't have him! Take me! Michael Archer was my father! The man who killed you! I'm his daughter!"

Eve let out a faint snarl, before letting go of Bradley's head and allowing him to fall down to the floor. Turning slowly, Eve looked at Debbie for a moment and then took a step forward.

"Let my son go, and you can kill me instead," Debbie said, her voice trembling with fear. "I'm -"

"His daughter?" Eve whispered, her voice icy and calm as she edged closer.

"I'm his daughter, yes," Debbie replied, unable to get up off her knees. "I only found out today, but Michael Archer viciously attacked my mother years ago, and I was the product of that. Michael Archer was a monster who hurt so many people in this town. You weren't his only victim, but you maybe suffered more than most. Still, his blood is in my veins, so if you really want to punish the man who killed you, I guess I'm as close as you're ever going to get."

Eve stopped, towering above her.

"His daughter," she whispered, before tilting her head slightly, "and his grandchild. Here."

"Forget my son," Debbie said through gritted teeth. "Open those doors and let him go, and I'll stay. I won't even fight, you can do whatever you want to me. That's what you're after, isn't it? You want revenge. So take it. For all the awful things that bastard Michael Archer did to you, go and -"

"He loved me!" she snarled angrily. "We were going to be happy!"

"He was nothing more than a monster and a -"

Before Debbie could get another word out, Eve grabbed the sides of her head and screamed, pressing her fingertips deep into her skull. Debbie let out an agonized gasp and tried in vain to pull away, but she was too weak and as blood began to run from her right nostril she could only look up at Eve and wait for death. She tried to cry out to Bradley, but at that moment she felt one of Eve's cold, sharp fingertips slicing through her cheek and slipping inside her mouth, cutting her tongue. The other fingertip ran straight down her cheek and cut through her chin, scraping the bone.

"No!" Bradley screamed. "Mum!"

CHAPTER THIRTY-THREE

"STOP!" A VOICE CALLED out, and suddenly the doors were flung open.

Turning, Bradley was shocked to see an old man limping into the hall, and he realized after a fraction of a second that somehow Michael Archer had arrived.

Michael took a couple of steps forward, before stopping as soon as he was able to make out the sight of Eve. Still holding Debbie's head, Eve looked at him and stayed strangely calm; she didn't seem to recognize him, necessarily, but he'd certainly caught her attention.

"Eve," Michael whispered, making his way over to join Bradley. "Is that really you?"

"You have to stop her!" Bradley said frantically. "She's killing my mum!"

"All the way here, I told myself that it wasn't possible," Michael replied, keeping his gaze firmly fixed on Eve. "It's a miracle my old car even started up, and another miracle that I managed to keep her on the road. I once swore that I'd never set foot in Crowford again, but the thought of seeing Eve again was too much. Is that *really* my beloved?"

Debbie let out a faint groan.

"Let go of her!" Bradley yelled at Eve. "You're hurting her!"

Eve looked down at Debbie for a moment, before pulling her hands away, letting her slump to the floor. Bradley rushed over to check on his mother, while Eve took a couple of cautious steps toward Michael.

"Are you okay?" Bradley asked, trying to help Debbie up. "Mum, say something!"

"If I'd known you were here," Michael said, watching as Eve approached, "I would have come here fifty years ago." There were tears in his eyes now. "If I'd thought that there was even a chance, I wouldn't have let anything stand between us."

"What happened?" Debbie groaned, as blood ran from her wounds.

Eve continued to make her way slowly toward Michael, and after a moment her expression began to soften a little, as if she finally recognized him after so many years.

"I was late," Michael continued. "It's all my fault. If I'd been on time, I would have been here to protect you. You have to believe me, I never meant to stay so long at the Crowford Farrier, but I just... I was a weak man back then, Eve. Maybe I still am now. I tried to hide that from you. I didn't even tell you my real name, I was too ashamed to admit that I was Michael Archer. I wanted to protect you from all the people who would have judged you if you'd told them who you were seeing. I didn't want your life to be in any way harmed by your association with me."

Eve tilted her head slightly, eyeing him with a mixture of caution and concern.

"It's me!" he said, taking a step closer. "What's wrong, don't you recognize me? It's Michael... Adam, as I wanted you to call me back then. I suppose the past fifty years haven't been kind to my features, have they? You'll have to forgive the fact that I look like an old man now, while you... I swear, it's as if you were frozen in time."

He hesitated, before slowly reaching out to her with his old, liver-spotted right hand.

"You remember me, don't you?" he asked, before looking around at the walls. "It sure looks like you do," he added, before turning to her again. His trembling hand was still outstretched, waiting for her touch. "Please, tell me that you remember the love we had. The love we can *still* have. I came back for you, my darling. After all these years, I've found you again."

"You..." she whispered.

"That's right. Me. Adam. Call me Michael now, though."

"You..."

He nodded.

He smiled.

"Murderer," she added.

"What?" He paused. "No, Eve, it wasn't "

"Murderer!" she screamed, lunging at him, grabbing his head and dragging him down to the floor as she let out a howl of pain. "You killed me!"

"No!" he gasped, trying in vain to push her away. "It wasn't me! You have to remember what happened! Didn't you see who really attacked you?"

"You murdered me and left me all alone in here," she sneered, as she began to rip her fingertips down through his face, as if she intended to scrape away all his flesh. "You lured me here and then you stabbed me in the back!"

"It wasn't me!" he groaned, as blood ran down across his features. "Please, try to remember..."

"I remember the knife in my back!" she snarled, leaning closer to him. "I remember the feel of it slicing through my heart!"

"We have to go," Debbie said, hauling herself up and dragging Bradley toward the door.

"She's insane. When she's done with him, she'll come back over to finish *us* off!"

"But he promised me he didn't kill her," Bradley replied, limping a little as they reached the door and looked back. "He was telling the truth, wasn't he?"

"I remember the pain," Eve continued, "as the blade was twisted. I remember the agony of the knife being driven into me again and again, and then..."

Her voice trailed off for a moment, as if she was reliving that awful time.

"And then I fell," she stammered, "and I looked back up, and I saw..."

Again, her voice faded.

"I saw..."

"It wasn't me," Michael sobbed. "You have to remember, my darling! I arrived later, after you were already dead. I was too late to do anything!"

"I saw..."

She froze for a moment, and then she began to sob as she ran her hands across Michael's bloodied face.

"It wasn't you!" she whimpered. "Adam, you came back to me! All these years, I thought it was you who killed me, but it wasn't! It never was!"

"I should have been there for you," he replied. "In some ways, I *did* kill you. You were my girl, and I let you down. I should have kept you safe."

"It wasn't your fault," she told him. "I see that now. When I first woke up here and realized I was dead, I felt so confused. I heard people talking, and all they said over and over was that everyone knew you'd were the one who'd murdered me. I suppose I just came to believe that eventually, even though deep down I should have remembered the truth." She paused. "That final moment is still so hard to recall. I remember looking up and seeing my killer. I know it wasn't you now, but I'm not sure that I..."

She paused, as if she was desperately trying to recall who she'd seen.

"Why can't I remember?" she sobbed after a few more seconds. "Why can't I remember the moment I died?"

"I'm here now," he told her.

"But why did people say that you were the one?" she asked. "Why would they spread lies about you?"

"It doesn't matter now, I -"

"Why did this whole town turn against you?" she growled angrily. "What gave them the right to drag your good name through the mud? They lied about you, and they didn't even bother trying to find out who *actually* murdered me! They did all those awful things, and for what? For the chance to lie to themselves and pretend that they no longer had to worry? For the opportunity to make themselves sound like better people?"

"Eve..."

"You!" she sneered, turning and looking at Debbie and Bradley, who were still watching from the doorway. "You're just like all the rest!"

"Run!" Debbie yelled, grabbing Bradley's hand and forcing him back along the corridor. "We have to get to the -"

Before she could finish, one of the doors up ahead swung open. Debbie slammed into it hard, letting out a faint cry, but she managed to keep going. A moment later, however, another door did the same thing, then another, as if all the doors in the corridor were suddenly trying to get in the way. Debbie and Bradley managed to slip between them, and once they reached the main staircase they began to hurry down to the hallway.

"No!" Eve's voice screamed. "You won't get away with it!"

In an instant, the wooden boards began to fall away from the stairs. Debbie and Bradley both fell, hurtling down the remainder of the steps until they slammed into the floor at the bottom. Even before they were able to get up, wooden panels were tearing themselves off the walls and flying through the air, crashing against Debbie as she struggled to drag her son toward the doors, which had shut themselves. Grabbing the handles, Debbie desperately tried to get the doors back open, as the entire hallway ripped itself apart and tried to use its broken shards as weapons. At the top of the stairs, Eve Marsh appeared and screamed.

"Let us go!" Debbie shouted, as the remains of the disintegrating hallway swirled around them both, and as splinters sliced across her face. "Please! You can't do this to us!"

CHAPTER THIRTY-FOUR

STUMBLING DOWN THE STEPS at the front of the building, hand-in-hand, Debbie and Bradley finally reached the yard, where they dropped to the ground and tried to get their breath back.

Turning, Bradley looked up toward the school's doors, just as they swung shut again. At the very last moment, in the blink of an eye, he was just able to see Eve Marsh's ghost still standing at the top of the main staircase.

"What happened?" he asked, turning to his mother. "How did you manage to get the doors open?"

"I think it was..."

She paused, struggling to breathe.

"I think it was Michael," she said finally. "I think at the last moment he must have persuaded her to let go of her anger. I don't know what else could have made her change her mind. It's okay, though. We're out now. Even if she changes he mind again, I don't think she can get to us."

She began to get up, but she immediately crashed back down, and she already knew that she was too weak to walk.

"Bradley," she said after a moment, "I have to tell you something."

"It's okay," he replied. "I'll help you get home."

"It's not that," she continued, as she felt the last of her strength starting to drain away. "Bradley, I lied to you. I wasn't in remission, not this time. I checked myself out of the hospital because I wanted to come home and spend some time with you. I hated the fact that I only saw you on the ward. I could see the writing on the wall, and I wanted to have one last normal week."

"What do you mean?" he asked. "You're going to get better."

She looked up at the school building for a moment, imagining Eve Marsh's ghost still trapped somewhere inside, and then she turned to him.

"Sweetheart," she said, with tears starting to run down her cheeks, "you're eleven years old and you have to hear this. You have to be prepared for the possibility that..."

Her voice trailed off.

"That you won't get better?" he asked.

"Bradley -"

"I already knew that," he told her, before swallowing hard. He, too, had tears in his eyes, and his bottom lip was starting to tremble. "I just didn't want to say it out loud."

"It's cold out here," she replied, trying again to sit up. "We should -"

Suddenly her arms buckled. Bradley managed to catch her, cradling her in his arms as they sat on the ground in the bare, cold yard. Michael Archer's beaten-up old car was parked nearby,

"I've got you," he told her, as he eased her down.

"I don't think I was ever going to get out again," she said, struggling now to keep her eyes open. "I know what I did was foolish, and I can't really defend myself, but I wanted so badly to be out one last time. And now, Bradley, you've got to promise me that you're going to be really brave. It's going to be tough, but you need to be strong, not only for yourself but also for Nana, and for your father too, and you have to -"

"I saved the tape," he replied, interrupting her. Sniffing back more tears, he held up what was left of the recorder, with part of the tape hanging out in a tangled mess. "Do you think someone can make it play again?"

"Are you listening to me, Bradley?"

"All the recording should still be on there," he continued, as more tears filled his eyes. "I think I'll be able to find someone who can do it, and then Michael's words can be heard by the whole town. We'll put history right." He looked toward the school. "What about Michael? Shouldn't we go back and try to find him?"

"I think he'll be fine. If he wants to come out, he will. But Bradley, you have to listen to me. There's not much time and I -"

"If he can't speak for himself, the tape will have to do," he replied, cutting her off yet again. "It's not fair if people always think that he was a really awful man. They should know the truth. That's what you always said, Mum, isn't it? That the truth should come out?"

"Absolutely," she said. "I guess he wasn't really my father after all. Someone else attacked Nana. Like everything else, it was just blamed on Michael."

"And -"

"Which is why I had to tell you the real reason I came home," she added, more firmly this time. "I thought I'd have a nice normal week, maybe two at a push. Instead, you dragged me along on a hell of an adventure, didn't you?"

Bradley opened his mouth to reply, but then he hesitated. He knew exactly what his mother was trying to say, and he knew that he couldn't deny the truth for a moment longer.

"What are you thinking?" she asked finally.

"Well, it's going to be okay, isn't it?" he said cautiously. "I mean, we saw a real ghost today, didn't we?"

"Apparently."

"So there's no reason to be scared," he continued. "Not if you think about it. Eve Marsh came back as a ghost, so obviously death isn't the end. She died over fifty years ago, but she didn't just snap out of existence. She stayed, and she was still able to talk to people and do things. If she could stick around, then anyone can. Even if something bad *did* happen, Mum, you'd come back and haunt me, wouldn't you?"

"I'm not sure that it's quite as easy as that."

"But you'd try, right?"

Debbie paused, not knowing quite what to say to her son.

"Sure," she told him, before thinking for a moment. "Hey, you know the church near here? The old one that doesn't get used much?"

He nodded.

"I've always really liked that memorial that's kind of set into the wall on the corner, by the road. Do you know the one I mean?"

"The one with the big cross?"

"Exactly. Well, I -"

Suddenly she started coughing, and it took her a moment to clear her throat. Even then, when she looked down at her trembling hands she saw that they were spattered with blood. She quickly wiped the blood away on the side of her jeans, but when she looked at Bradley she could tell that he'd seen.

"If I *can* come back," she continued, "if there's any way at all, then that's where I'll be. So any time you go past that cross, take a look and if it's at all possible, I'll be next to it and I'll wave at you."

"Can't you haunt the house instead?"

"I don't want to linger like a stale fart," she replied. She began to laugh, but then she let out a gasp as she felt a sharp pain in her chest. "This is a compromise, okay?" she added. "I'll be next to that cross."

"How will you know when I'm going to come past?" he asked. "Will you have to stand there all the time, just in case?"

"I imagine there'll be some way for me to know," she told him, and she could feel herself getting weaker by the second, as if the last of her strength was finally leaving her body. "Hey, do me a favor. Can you go and get help? There's a payphone at the front of the school's new building, isn't there?"

"I think so."

Reaching into her pocket, she pulled out a fifty pence coin and handed it to him.

"Call Nana," she said. "You know the number, don't you?"

"Of course."

"Then call Nana and tell her to call the police. Tell her not to be too mad at you, tell her I said that."

"Can't you tell her all of that?"

"Maybe, sweetheart," she said as her eyes began to close. "I'll be fine here. Don't worry about me. Go and make that phone call and... I'll just wait... right..."

Her voice trailed off.

"Here," she added finally, followed by a long sigh.

Still holding her, Bradley waited for her to continue. He wanted to ask her if she was okay, to maybe shake her a little, but he was too scared to do anything in case she didn't respond. He knew exactly where to find the payphone, and he supposed that he'd have to go over there eventually, but he wasn't too cold so he decided to wait just a little while longer. And so, sitting in the shadow of the old school building, he sat with his mother and tried to work out exactly how he was going to be brave. Sure, he'd entered a haunted house and survived an encounter with a vengeful ghost, and he'd gone to a remote farmhouse and faced down a man he'd thought was a murderer, and those things had been brave to some degree.

He was starting to realize, however, that soon he was going to have to be so much braver still.

CHAPTER THIRTY-FIVE

Four weeks later...

STILL WEARING THE SMART little suit that his grandmother had picked out for him, Bradley stepped out of the car and took a deep breath. The early summer air was warm and full, and nearby trees were rustling in the rays of a warm day. Bradley watched as a squirrel scurried up one of the trees, and then he turned and looked over at the school building.

"Are you sure about this?" his father asked. "Bradley, it's good to be conscientious, but you *are* allowed to take the rest of today off. I mean, after this morning..."

"No, I want to come to school," he replied, grabbing his bag from the car. "I'll change in the changing room, and then I'll go to class."

"Bradley, there's really no shame in just coming home with us. The funeral was tough, and you might be better off just trying to relax."

"It's almost the end of the term," he pointed out, "and soon we're going to go to secondary school. I don't want to miss even a single day, not if I don't have to. Besides, this afternoon we're going to watch the demolition, and I can't miss that, not for anything."

"Okay, well, if you're sure..." His father hesitated for a moment. "She'd be proud of you, you know. Not just for today, but for everything."

"I know," he replied, before swinging the door shut. "Are you picking me up after school?"

"You'd better believe it," Dave said. "And, hey, we'll go for ice cream."

"We don't have to if you don't want to."

"Are you kidding? I want ice cream, so we're having ice cream. There's really no room for debate."

Turning, Bradley made his way toward the front door. There was a part of him that had wanted to stay home for the rest of the day, but deep down he knew that he had some unfinished business. Already, up ahead, he could see a group of workers in hardhats standing near the main reception, chatting away as they prepared for their big job.

***

A few minutes later, once he'd changed into his uniform, Bradley set out across the field. He could see all his classmates up ahead, gathering behind the safety barrier to watch the big moment, and he picked up the pace to make sure that he'd join them in time.

Debbie had gone back into hospital after the night at the old school. She'd been much weaker by then, but she'd survived for another week and a half, gradually slipping away day by day. The doctors had admitted that, all things considered, her trip home probably hadn't hastened matters very much. Bradley had been by her side for the final moment, and he'd felt her last breath. He and his mother hadn't talked much about what had happened in the school; Debbie hadn't really had the strength to talk to anyone. The police had eventually stopped asking questions, apparently preferring to honor the town's long tradition of sweeping uncomfortable truths under the carpet.

The damaged tape remained un-repaired, but Bradley felt certain that he'd get to its contents one day.

Ahead, the wrecking ball was already being maneuvered into position.

Bradley had tried to tell people that Michael Archer wasn't to blame for everything that had happened. Some people had seemed willing to consider the possibility, but most had been unmoved and had simply been glad that this time he was definitely dead. After all, his body had been found in the school, along with Lou's. The tape would hopefully change things one day, but Bradley and his mother had at least managed to get Josephine to accept the news. Having long believe that Michael had been the one who'd attacked her, Josephine had been forced to come to terms with the fact that the real attacker would likely never be identified. She'd taken the news in her stride, and she'd quickly come to focus instead on tending to Debbie's needs in those final days.

Reaching the back of the crowd, Bradley quickly managed to find Christian and Simon.

"How was it?" Christian asked.

"It was okay," Bradley said, craning his neck to get a better view of what was about to happen. The demolition of the old school had been delayed a little by the police investigation, but now it was ready to go ahead. "What's happening here?"

"They're going to smash that place down and turn it into rubble," Simon said keenly. "I've never seen an actual wrecking ball before!"

"Will everyone please calm down?" Mr. Kepper called out, clearly irritated. "You're all supposed to be taking notes, remember? We're not here for fun, we're here to learn something!"

"Yes, Mr. Kepper," about half the crowd murmured.

Glancing to his left, Bradley saw Charles standing a little way back, all alone. Ever since his encounter in the old school, Charles hadn't been the same; his usual sense of humor had seemingly drained deserted him, and he seemed nervy and twitchy. Bradley and the others had tried a few times to get through to him, never with any luck, but Bradley was convinced that eventually he'd manage to admit the truth. As Charles turned and saw that he was being watched, Bradley offered a nervous smile, but Charles simply looked back over at the old school.

Finally, the wrecking ball was ready and everyone fell quiet. A kind of tense anticipation was rippling through the crowd. The entire school was ready to see the old building get completely destroyed.

A moment later, a cry rang out and the ball swung, crashing through one of the upstairs sections. Everyone began to cheer as chunks of wood and stone rained down, and soon the ball was sent swinging again, this time ripping out an even bigger section of the building.

"This is so cool!" Christian gasped. "Look! You can see inside!"

As the ball smashed away another section, Bradley saw that he was right. One side of the old hall had been destroyed, leaving the rest – including part of the balcony and the stage – exposed to bright daylight. Bradley felt a little strange as he saw the exact spot where the ghost of Eve Marsh had attacked him; that hall had seemed so scary and ominous at night, but now it was just another room. And then, as the ball smashed through the building again, the last of the hall collapsed in a shower of dust and debris.

Bradley started looking at the few remaining windows. He'd been expecting to maybe see some hint of Eve Marsh's ghost, although he figured that might be unlikely. After a couple of seconds, however, he realized he could see a face at the farthest window. He looked around and realized that nobody else had noticed, and when he looked back up he saw not one but two faces staring out from the old building.

Eve Marsh and Michael Archer looked so calm as they stared down at Bradley.

Before he could say anything, Bradley saw the wrecking ball smash straight through that last part of the building. The ghosts of Eve and Michael disappeared in an instant as the final chunk of the school's upper section collapsed. Michael couldn't help thinking that the ghostly figures had looked strangely content, as if they'd finally been released from their hellish tragedy.

"Alright, everyone," Mr. Kepper said, "back

to class. Come on, you lot, move it!"

With most of the work complete, everyone began to head back across the field.

"I know this might sound weird," Christian said, "but I wouldn't want to live in any of the flats that get built on that land."

"Why not?" Simon asked.

"Why do you think? It might still be haunted! What if you bought a brand new flat, and then you found that the ghost of Eve Marsh was still there?"

"I'm pretty sure she won't be," Bradley replied.

"Hey, what about your mum?" Christian asked. "You said she promised to try to appear to you, right? Wasn't she going to be at that cross outside the church?"

"That's what she told me. If she could."

"Well?"

"We've been past a few times," Bradley told him. "I always look, but there's no sign of her."

"That sucks," Christian said. "Sorry, dude. You must be really disappointed."

"Actually, I'm not," he replied, as Mr. Kepper shouted at them all to hurry up. "I think maybe ghosts only turn up if the person who died was sad, or if they had unfinished business. If she isn't appearing, that means my mum doesn't feel that way. Nana says she's watching over me, and that's probably true, but I don't think she's hanging around like..." He paused. "Like a stale fart."

Christian and Simon laughed.

"After all," Bradley continued, turning and looking back at the cloud of dust that marked the spot where the old school had once stood, "who ever heard of a happy ghost?"

EPILOGUE

ONE WEEK LATER, sitting on the grass at lunchtime, Bradley watched for a moment as the builders worked on the site where the new flats were going to be built.

"So this is it," Christian said, "our last lunchtime ever. At this school, at least."

"Relax," Simon replied, "we're all going to the same secondary school. We'll have plenty more lunchtimes together starting in September."

"That's easy to say now," Christian pointed out, "but what if one of us turns into a jerk?"

"Why would we do that?" Bradley asked.

"I don't know, but I see kids from the secondary school in town and a lot of *them* are jerks. And they probably don't mean for it to happen, either. It's probably random. In which case, any one of us could turn into one."

"I'm not sure that's how it works," Bradley told him.

"Well, *I* promise not to be a jerk," Simon said. "I don't think I have much potential to be a jerk, anyway. Just in case, though, I want you two to let me know if you see the early signs."

"Ditto," Bradley said.

"Me too," Christian added, reaching out with his right hand. "We'll protect each other from becoming jerks. Deal?"

They all shook on the arrangement.

"You know," Christian continued, "there's still one thing that's bothering me about the whole Eve Marsh thing. I know it's unrealistic for us to expect to get answers to all our questions. Life just doesn't work that way. But now we know that Michael Archer didn't kill Eve, are we ever going to find out who the real murderer was?"

"Whoever did it," Bradley replied, "has most likely been dead for years."

"I know, but don't you have this insane sense of curiosity?"

"Sure," Bradley said, "but I don't know what we can do about it. Even Eve herself didn't seem to remember, not even right at the end. It was as if the moment of her own death was wiped from her mind."

"So it's going to remain a mystery forever?"

Christian said. "That sucks."

"It *totally* sucks," Simon added.

"It's just the way it is," Bradley told them. "I suppose we just have to accept that real life isn't as neat as stories. We got most of the answers, but a few slipped away. We're never going to find out who really killed Eve Marsh."

***

September 10th, 1936...

"Adam," Eve Marsh said cautiously, "I think -"

Suddenly she let out a pained gasp as a knife burst into her back and out through the center of her chest. Looking down, she saw the tip glinting in the low light, and blood was already dripping down from the blade. She tried to cry out, but somehow she found that she could barely make a sound at all, and she realized she could feel blood soaking the front of her dress. And then, just as she managed to let out a faint groan, she felt another sharp pain as the knife was twisted from behind.

"No!" she sobbed, already feeling the life drain from her body as her knees began to buckle. "Please, no..."

The attacker pulled the knife out, before driving it into Eve's back several more times. Dropping to the floor, Eve froze for a moment as she felt more blood soaking her dress, and then she collapsed onto her side. Gasping for breath and already feeling weaker, she rolled onto her back and tried to get up, but then she saw a silhouetted figure standing over her. A moment later, the figure took a step forward, and Eve finally saw the face of the killer.

"What?" she stammered, recognizing one of her former pupils. "I don't..."

Still holding the bloodied knife, the girl – who had only recently celebrated her seventeenth birthday – stared down at her victim and allowed herself a faint smile.

"You!" Eve gasped. "Why?"

The girl hesitated, before opening her mouth to reply.

"Vivian?" Angela Grace shouted, suddenly rushing into the hall and then stopping as soon as she saw the awful scene. "No! Vivian, what have you done?"

"Vivian Grace," Eve stammered, as blood ran from one corner of her mouth, "why would you do this to me?"

"Because you have something I want," Vivian replied coldly. "I know you've been meeting Mr. Archer, and I don't think you're right for him. You're not pretty enough, and you're not clever enough, and you're just all round not good enough for a handsome man like him. He deserves nothing but the best!"

"Vivian, you shouldn't have done this," Angela said, stepping up behind her and carefully taking the knife from her sister's hand. "Oh Vivian, I knew Mr. Archer was your latest fancy, but I had no idea you were going to do something like this!"

"He's not my latest fancy!" Vivian snapped. "I really love him!"

"You've barely ever spoken to him," Angela pointed out. "I'm not sure he even knows who you are. You know what you're like, you'll be into someone different next week."

"The bitch was coming here to meet him tonight," Vivian sneered, as Eve sobbed on the floor. "Look at her, writhing in agony down there like a gutted fish. What kind of whore meets a man late at night in a place like this, anyway? Come on, let's get out of here."

"She's dying," Angela whispered, stepping past Vivian and looking down at Eve. "She's suffering. We can't leave her like this."

Gasping desperately for air, Eve began to shake violently.

"I'm so sorry," Angela said, dropping to her knees, still holding the knife. "I didn't know she was going to do anything like this. She just gets obsessed by things, you see, and then she gets angry if she can't have them. She's always been like that, I've tried to hold her back, but sometimes..."

Eve tried to say something, but all that emerged from her mouth was more blood.

"I'll stop the pain for you," Angela continued, holding the tip of the blade against Eve's chest. "That's really all I can do now. You must forgive me, I'm only trying to do the right thing."

"Please," Eve gasped, "I -"

Closing her eyes tight, Angela pushed the knife deep into Eve's body. She immediately pulled it out and threw it aside, before stumbling to her feet and taking a step back. Eve had fallen still, save for a faint tremor that was causing her lips to slightly move.

"I'm sorry," Angela said, with tears in her eyes, before taking Vivian's hand and leading her out of the room. "Come on, we have to leave before anyone finds us here. No-one must ever be allowed to know what you did. Oh Vivian, why do you get like this? What am I ever going to do about you? We can't let Father know, of course. We shall just have to make sure that he truth never gets out."

"I don't see why you're making such a fuss," Vivian replied. "She was only a teacher."

As the voices and footsteps receded into the distance, Eve Marsh lay on the floor and felt her life drain away. She was staring up into the darkness, and she already knew that she had no hope of surviving. She could feel blood running out of her body, and she could no longer even remember how to breathe. All she could do was wait for the end, as dust drifted down and landed on her skin, and she thought of her dear Adam as the last light of life finally faded from her dead eyes.

Also in this series

THE HAUNTING OF NELSON STREET
(THE GHOSTS OF CROWFORD BOOK 1)

Crowford, a sleepy coastal town in the south of England, might seem like an oasis of calm and tranquility. Beneath the surface, however, dark secrets are waiting to claim fresh victims, and ghostly figures plot revenge.

Having finally decided to leave the hustle of London, Daisy and Richard Johnson buy two houses on Nelson Street, a picturesque street in the center of Crowford. One house is perfect and ready to move into, while the other is a fire-ravaged wreck that needs a lot of work. They figure they have plenty of time to work on the damaged house while Daisy recovers from a traumatic event.

Soon, they discover that the two houses share a common link to the past. Something awful once happened on Nelson Street, something that shook the town to its core.

AMY CROSS

Also in this series

THE GHOST OF CROWFORD SCHOOL
(THE GHOSTS OF CROWFORD BOOK 2)

The year is 1950, and a great tragedy has struck the town of Crowford. Three local men have been killed in a storm, after their fishing boat the Mercy Belle sank. A mysterious fourth man, however, was rescue. Nobody knows who he is, or what he was doing on the Mercy Belle... and the man has lost his memory.

Five years later, messages from the dead warn of impending doom for Crowford. The ghosts of the Mercy Belle's crew demand revenge, and the whole town is being punished. The fourth man still has no memory of his previous existence, but he's married now and living under the named Edward Smith. As Crowford's suffering continues, the locals begin to turn against him.

What really happened on the night the Mercy Belle sank? Did the fourth man cause the tragedy? And will Crowford survive if this man is not sent to meet his fate?

AMY CROSS

Also by Amy Cross

The Devil, the Witch and the Whore
(The Deal book 1)

"Leave the forest alone. Whatever's out there, just let it be. Don't make it angry."

When a horrific discovery is made at the edge of town, Sheriff James Kopperud realizes the answers he seeks might be waiting beyond in the vast forest. But everybody in the town of Deal knows that there's something out there in the forest, something that should never be disturbed. A deal was made long ago, a deal that was supposed to keep the town safe. And if he insists on investigating the murder of a local girl, James is going to have to break that deal and head out into the wilderness.

Meanwhile, James has no idea that his estranged daughter Ramsey has returned to town. Ramsey is running from something, and she thinks she can find safety in the vast tunnel system that runs beneath the forest. Before long, however, Ramsey finds herself coming face to face with creatures that hide in the shadows. One of these creatures is known as the devil, and another is known as the witch. They're both waiting for the whore to arrive, but for very different reasons. And soon Ramsey is offered a terrible deal, one that could save or destroy the entire town, and maybe even the world.

Also by Amy Cross

The Soul Auction

"I saw a woman on the beach. I watched her face a demon."

Thirty years after her mother's death, Alice Ashcroft is drawn back to the coastal English town of Curridge. Somebody in Curridge has been reviewing Alice's novels online, and in those reviews there have been tantalizing hints at a hidden truth. A truth that seems to be linked to her dead mother.

"Thirty years ago, there was a soul auction."

Once she reaches Curridge, Alice finds strange things happening all around her. Something attacks her car. A figure watches her on the beach at night. And when she tries to find the person who has been reviewing her books, she makes a horrific discovery.

What really happened to Alice's mother thirty years ago? Who was she talking to, just moments before dropping dead on the beach? What caused a huge rockfall that nearly tore a nearby cliff-face in half? And what sinister presence is lurking in the grounds of the local church?

Also by Amy Cross

Darper Danver: The Complete First Series

Five years ago, three friends went to a remote cabin in the woods and tried to contact the spirit of a long-dead soldier. They thought they could control whatever happened next. They were wrong...

Newly released from prison, Cassie Briggs returns to Fort Powell, determined to get her life back on track. Soon, however, she begins to suspect that an ancient evil still lurks in the nearby cabin. Was the mysterious Darper Danver really destroyed all those years ago, or does her spirit still linger, waiting for a chance to return?

As Cassie and her ex-boyfriend Fisher are finally forced to face the truth about what happened in the cabin, they realize that Darper isn't ready to let go of their lives just yet. Meanwhile, a vengeful woman plots revenge for her brother's murder, and a New York ghost writer arrives in town to uncover the truth. Before long, strange carvings begin to appear around town and blood starts to flow once again.

AMY CROSS

Also by Amy Cross

The Ghost of Molly Holt

"Molly Holt is dead. There's nothing to fear in this house."

When three teenagers set out to explore an abandoned house in the middle of a forest, they think they've found the location where the infamous Molly Holt video was filmed.

They've found much more than that...

Tim doesn't believe in ghosts, but he has a crush on a girl who does. That's why he ends up taking her out to the house, and it's also why he lets her take his only flashlight. But as they explore the house together, Tim and Becky start to realize that something else might be lurking in the shadows.

Something that, ten years ago, suffered unimaginable pain.

Something that won't rest until a terrible wrong has been put right.

Also by Amy Cross

American Coven

He kidnapped three women and held them in his basement. He thought they couldn't fight back. He was wrong...

Snatched from the street near her home, Holly Carter is taken to a rural house and thrown down into a stone basement. She meets two other women who have also been kidnapped, and soon Holly learns about the horrific rituals that take place in the house. Eventually, she's called upstairs to take her place in the ice bath.

As her nightmare continues, however, Holly learns about a mysterious power that exists in the basement, and which the three women might be able to harness. When they finally manage to get through the metal door, however, the women have no idea that their fight for freedom is going to stretch out for more than a decade, or that it will culminate in a final, devastating demonstration of their new-found powers.

AMY CROSS

Also by Amy Cross

The Ash House

Why would anyone ever return to a haunted house?

For Diane Mercer the answer is simple. She's dying of cancer, and she wants to know once and for all whether ghosts are real.

Heading home with her young son, Diane is determined to find out whether the stories are real. After all, everyone else claimed to see and hear strange things in the house over the years. Everyone except Diane had some kind of experience in the house, or in the little ash house in the yard.

As Diane explores the house where she grew up, however, her son is exploring the yard and the forest. And while his mother might be struggling to come to terms with her own impending death, Daniel Mercer is puzzled by fleeting appearances of a strange little girl who seems drawn to the ash house, and by strange, rasping coughs that he keeps hearing at night.

The Ash House is a horror novel about a woman who desperately wants to know what will happen to her when she dies, and about a boy who uncovers the shocking truth about a young girl's murder.

Also by Amy Cross

Haunted

Twenty years ago, the ghost of a dead little girl drove Sheriff Michael Blaine to his death.

Now, that same ghost is coming for his daughter.

Returning to the small town where she grew up, Alex Roberts is determined to live a normal, quiet life. For the residents of Railham, however, she's an unwelcome reminder of the town's darkest hour.

Twenty years ago, nine-year-old Mo Garvey was found brutally murdered in a nearby forest. Everyone thinks that Alex's father was responsible, but if the killer was brought to justice, why is the ghost of Mo Garvey still after revenge?

And how far will the real killer go to protect his secret, when Alex starts getting closer to the truth?

Haunted is a horror novel about a woman who has to face her past, about a town that would rather forget, and about a little girl who refuses to let death stand in her way.

AMY CROSS

Also by Amy Cross

The Curse of Wetherley House

"If you walk through that door, Evil Mary will get you."

When she agrees to visit a supposedly haunted house with an old friend, Rosie assumes she'll encounter nothing more scary than a few creaks and bumps in the night. Even the legend of Evil Mary doesn't put her off. After all, she knows ghosts aren't real. But when Mary makes her first appearance, Rosie realizes she might already be trapped.

For more than a century, Wetherley House has been cursed. A horrific encounter on a remote road in the late 1800's has already caused a chain of misery and pain for all those who live at the house. Wetherley House was abandoned long ago, after a terrible discovery in the basement, something has remained undetected within its room. And even the local children know that Evil Mary waits in the house for anyone foolish enough to walk through the front door.

Before long, Rosie realizes that her entire life has been defined by the spirit of a woman who died in agony. Can she become the first person to escape Evil Mary, or will she fall victim to the same fate as the house's other occupants?

AMY CROSS

Also by Amy Cross

The Ghosts of Hexley Airport

Ten years ago, more than two hundred people died in a horrific plane crash at Hexley Airport.

Today, some say their ghosts still haunt the terminal building.

When she starts her new job at the airport, working a night shift as part of the security team, Casey assumes the stories about the place can't be true. Even when she has a strange encounter in a deserted part of the departure hall, she's certain that ghosts aren't real.

Soon, however, she's forced to face the truth. Not only is there something haunting the airport's buildings and tarmac, but a sinister force is working behind the scenes to replicate the circumstances of the original accident. And as a snowstorm moves in, Hexley Airport looks set to witness yet another disaster.

AMY CROSS

Also by Amy Cross

The Girl Who Never Came Back

Twenty years ago, Charlotte Abernathy vanished while playing near her family's house. Despite a frantic search, no trace of her was found until a year later, when the little girl turned up on the doorstep with no memory of where she'd been.

Today, Charlotte has put her mysterious ordeal behind her, even though she's never learned where she was during that missing year. However, when her eight-year-old niece vanishes in similar circumstances, a fully-grown Charlotte is forced to make a fresh attempt to uncover the truth.

Originally published in 2013, the fully revised and updated version of *The Girl Who Never Came Back* tells the harrowing story of a woman who thought she could forget her past, and of a little girl caught in the tangled web of a dark family secret.

AMY CROSS

Also by Amy Cross

Asylum
(The Asylum Trilogy book 1)

"No-one ever leaves Lakehurst. The staff, the patients, the ghosts... Once you're here, you're stuck forever."

After shooting her little brother dead, Annie Radford is sent to Lakehurst psychiatric hospital for assessment. Hearing voices in her head, Annie is forced to undergo experimental new treatments devised by a mysterious old man who lives in the hospital's attic. It soon becomes clear that the hospital's staff, led by the vicious Nurse Winter, are hiding something horrific at Lakehurst.

As Annie struggles to survive the hospital, she learns more about Nurse Winter's own story. Once a promising young medical student, Kirsten Winter also heard voices in her head. Voices that traveled a long way to reach her. Voices that have a plan of their own. Voices that will stop at nothing to get what they want.

What kind of signals are being transmitted from the basement of the hospital? Who is the old man in the attic? Why are living human brains kept in jars? And what is the dark secret that lurks at the heart of the hospital?

AMY CROSS

BOOKS BY AMY CROSS

1. Dark Season: The Complete First Series (2011)
2. Werewolves of Soho (Lupine Howl book 1) (2012)
3. Werewolves of the Other London (Lupine Howl book 2) (2012)
4. Ghosts: The Complete Series (2012)
5. Dark Season: The Complete Second Series (2012)
6. The Children of Black Annis (Lupine Howl book 3) (2012)
7. Destiny of the Last Wolf (Lupine Howl book 4) (2012)
8. Asylum (The Asylum Trilogy book 1) (2012)
9. Dark Season: The Complete Third Series (2013)
10. Devil's Briar (2013)
11. Broken Blue (The Broken Trilogy book 1) (2013)
12. The Night Girl (2013)
13. Days 1 to 4 (Mass Extinction Event book 1) (2013)
14. Days 5 to 8 (Mass Extinction Event book 2) (2013)
15. The Library (The Library Chronicles book 1) (2013)
16. American Coven (2013)
17. Werewolves of Sangreth (Lupine Howl book 5) (2013)
18. Broken White (The Broken Trilogy book 2) (2013)
19. Grave Girl (Grave Girl book 1) (2013)
20. Other People's Bodies (2013)
21. The Shades (2013)
22. The Vampire's Grave and Other Stories (2013)
23. Darper Danver: The Complete First Series (2013)
24. The Hollow Church (2013)
25. The Dead and the Dying (2013)
26. Days 9 to 16 (Mass Extinction Event book 3) (2013)
27. The Girl Who Never Came Back (2013)
28. Ward Z (The Ward Z Series book 1) (2013)
29. Journey to the Library (The Library Chronicles book 2) (2014)
30. The Vampires of Tor Cliff Asylum (2014)
31. The Family Man (2014)
32. The Devil's Blade (2014)
33. The Immortal Wolf (Lupine Howl book 6) (2014)
34. The Dying Streets (Detective Laura Foster book 1) (2014)
35. The Stars My Home (2014)
36. The Ghost in the Rain and Other Stories (2014)
37. Ghosts of the River Thames (The Robinson Chronicles book 1) (2014)
38. The Wolves of Cur'eath (2014)
39. Days 46 to 53 (Mass Extinction Event book 4) (2014)
40. The Man Who Saw the Face of the World (2014)

AMY CROSS

41. The Art of Dying (Detective Laura Foster book 2) (2014)
42. Raven Revivals (Grave Girl book 2) (2014)
43. Arrival on Thaxos (Dead Souls book 1) (2014)
44. Birthright (Dead Souls book 2) (2014)
45. A Man of Ghosts (Dead Souls book 3) (2014)
46. The Haunting of Hardstone Jail (2014)
47. A Very Respectable Woman (2015)
48. Better the Devil (2015)
49. The Haunting of Marshall Heights (2015)
50. Terror at Camp Everbee (The Ward Z Series book 2) (2015)
51. Guided by Evil (Dead Souls book 4) (2015)
52. Child of a Bloodied Hand (Dead Souls book 5) (2015)
53. Promises of the Dead (Dead Souls book 6) (2015)
54. Days 54 to 61 (Mass Extinction Event book 5) (2015)
55. Angels in the Machine (The Robinson Chronicles book 2) (2015)
56. The Curse of Ah-Qal's Tomb (2015)
57. Broken Red (The Broken Trilogy book 3) (2015)
58. The Farm (2015)
59. Fallen Heroes (Detective Laura Foster book 3) (2015)
60. The Haunting of Emily Stone (2015)
61. Cursed Across Time (Dead Souls book 7) (2015)
62. Destiny of the Dead (Dead Souls book 8) (2015)
63. The Death of Jennifer Kazakos (Dead Souls book 9) (2015)
64. Alice Isn't Well (Death Herself book 1) (2015)
65. Annie's Room (2015)
66. The House on Everley Street (Death Herself book 2) (2015)
67. Meds (The Asylum Trilogy book 2) (2015)
68. Take Me to Church (2015)
69. Ascension (Demon's Grail book 1) (2015)
70. The Priest Hole (Nykolas Freeman book 1) (2015)
71. Eli's Town (2015)
72. The Horror of Raven's Briar Orphanage (Dead Souls book 10) (2015)
73. The Witch of Thaxos (Dead Souls book 11) (2015)
74. The Rise of Ashalla (Dead Souls book 12) (2015)
75. Evolution (Demon's Grail book 2) (2015)
76. The Island (The Island book 1) (2015)
77. The Lighthouse (2015)
78. The Cabin (The Cabin Trilogy book 1) (2015)
79. At the Edge of the Forest (2015)
80. The Devil's Hand (2015)
81. The 13th Demon (Demon's Grail book 3) (2016)
82. After the Cabin (The Cabin Trilogy book 2) (2016)
83. The Border: The Complete Series (2016)
84. The Dead Ones (Death Herself book 3) (2016)

85. A House in London (2016)
86. Persona (The Island book 2) (2016)
87. Battlefield (Nykolas Freeman book 2) (2016)
88. Perfect Little Monsters and Other Stories (2016)
89. The Ghost of Shapley Hall (2016)
90. The Blood House (2016)
91. The Death of Addie Gray (2016)
92. The Girl With Crooked Fangs (2016)
93. Last Wrong Turn (2016)
94. The Body at Auercliff (2016)
95. The Printer From Hell (2016)
96. The Dog (2016)
97. The Nurse (2016)
98. The Haunting of Blackwych Grange (2016)
99. Twisted Little Things and Other Stories (2016)
100. The Horror of Devil's Root Lake (2016)
101. The Disappearance of Katie Wren (2016)
102. B&B (2016)
103. The Bride of Ashbyrn House (2016)
104. The Devil, the Witch and the Whore (The Deal Trilogy book 1) (2016)
105. The Ghosts of Lakeforth Hotel (2016)
106. The Ghost of Longthorn Manor and Other Stories (2016)
107. Laura (2017)
108. The Murder at Skellin Cottage (Jo Mason book 1) (2017)
109. The Curse of Wetherley House (2017)
110. The Ghosts of Hexley Airport (2017)
111. The Return of Rachel Stone (Jo Mason book 2) (2017)
112. Haunted (2017)
113. The Vampire of Downing Street and Other Stories (2017)
114. The Ash House (2017)
115. The Ghost of Molly Holt (2017)
116. The Camera Man (2017)
117. The Soul Auction (2017)
118. The Abyss (The Island book 3) (2017)
119. Broken Window (The House of Jack the Ripper book 1) (2017)
120. In Darkness Dwell (The House of Jack the Ripper book 2) (2017)
121. Cradle to Grave (The House of Jack the Ripper book 3) (2017)
122. The Lady Screams (The House of Jack the Ripper book 4) (2017)
123. A Beast Well Tamed (The House of Jack the Ripper book 5) (2017)
124. Doctor Charles Grazier (The House of Jack the Ripper book 6) (2017)
125. The Raven Watcher (The House of Jack the Ripper book 7) (2017)
126. The Final Act (The House of Jack the Ripper book 8) (2017)
127. Stephen (2017)
128. The Spider (2017)

AMY CROSS

129. The Mermaid's Revenge (2017)
130. The Girl Who Threw Rocks at the Devil (2018)
131. Friend From the Internet (2018)
132. Beautiful Familiar (2018)
133. One Night at a Soul Auction (2018)
134. 16 Frames of the Devil's Face (2018)
135. The Haunting of Caldgrave House (2018)
136. Like Stones on a Crow's Back (The Deal Trilogy book 2) (2018)
137. Room 9 and Other Stories (2018)
138. The Gravest Girl of All (Grave Girl book 3) (2018)
139. Return to Thaxos (Dead Souls book 13) (2018)
140. The Madness of Annie Radford (The Asylum Trilogy book 3) (2018)
141. The Haunting of Briarwych Church (Briarwych book 1) (2018)
142. I Just Want You To Be Happy (2018)
143. Day 100 (Mass Extinction Event book 6) (2018)
144. The Horror of Briarwych Church (Briarwych book 2) (2018)
145. The Ghost of Briarwych Church (Briarwych book 3) (2018)
146. Lights Out (2019)
147. Apocalypse (The Ward Z Series book 3) (2019)
148. Days 101 to 108 (Mass Extinction Event book 7) (2019)
149. The Haunting of Daniel Bayliss (2019)
150. The Purchase (2019)
151. Harper's Hotel Ghost Girl (Death Herself book 4) (2019)
152. The Haunting of Aldburn House (2019)
153. Days 109 to 116 (Mass Extinction Event book 8) (2019)
154. Bad News (2019)
155. The Wedding of Rachel Blaine (2019)
156. Dark Little Wonders and Other Stories (2019)
157. The Music Man (2019)
158. The Vampire Falls (Three Nights of the Vampire book 1) (2019)
159. The Other Ann (2019)
160. The Butcher's Husband and Other Stories (2019)
161. The Haunting of Lannister Hall (2019)
162. The Vampire Burns (Three Nights of the Vampire book 2) (2019)
163. Days 195 to 202 (Mass Extinction Event book 9) (2019)
164. Escape From Hotel Necro (2019)
165. The Vampire Rises (Three Nights of the Vampire book 3) (2019)
166. Ten Chimes to Midnight: A Collection of Ghost Stories (2019)
167. The Strangler's Daughter (2019)
168. The Beast on the Tracks (2019)
169. The Haunting of the King's Head (2019)
170. I Married a Serial Killer (2019)
171. Your Inhuman Heart (2020)
172. Days 203 to 210 (Mass Extinction Event book 10) (2020)

173. The Ghosts of David Brook (2020)
174. Days 349 to 356 (Mass Extinction Event book 11) (2020)
175. The Horror at Criven Farm (2020)
176. Mary (2020)
177. The Middlewych Experiment (Chaos Gear Annie book 1) (2020)
178. Days 357 to 364 (Mass Extinction Event book 12) (2020)
179. Day 365: The Final Day (Mass Extinction Event book 13) (2020)
180. The Haunting of Hathaway House (2020)
181. Don't Let the Devil Know Your Name (2020)
182. The Legend of Rinth (2020)
183. The Ghost of Old Coal House (2020)
184. The Root (2020)
185. I'm Not a Zombie (2020)
186. The Ghost of Annie Close (2020)
187. The Disappearance of Lonnie James (2020)
188. The Curse of the Langfords (2020)
189. The Haunting of Nelson Street (The Ghosts of Crowford 1) (2020)
190. Strange Little Horrors and Other Stories (2020)
191. The House Where She Died (2020)
192. The Revenge of the Mercy Belle (The Ghosts of Crowford 2) (2020)

AMY CROSS

For more information, visit:

www.blackwychbooks.com

AMY CROSS

Printed in Dunstable, United Kingdom